MURDER
WITH A PAST

MURDER WITH A PAST

ELLERY QUEEN

THORNDIKE
CHIVERS

This Large Print edition is published by Thorndike Press®, Waterville, Maine USA and by BBC Audiobooks, Ltd, Bath, England.

Published in 2003 in the U.S. by arrangement with JackTime.

Published in 2003 in the U.K. by arrangement with The Frederic Dannay Literary Property Trust & The Manfred B. Lee Family Literary Property Trust.

U.S. Softcover 0-7862-6046-7 (Paperback)
U.K. Hardcover 0-7540-7775-6 (Chivers Large Print)
U.K. Softcover 0-7540-7776-4 (Camden Large Print)

The text of this Large Print edition is unabridged.
Other aspects of the book may vary from the original edition.

Set in 16 pt. Plantin.

Printed in the United States on permanent paper.

=====

British Library Cataloguing-in-Publication Data available

=====

Library of Congress Cataloging-in-Publication Data

Queen, Ellery.
    Murder with a past / Ellery Queen.
        p. cm.
    ISBN 0-7862-6046-7 (lg. print : sc : alk. paper)
    1. Fugitives from justice — Fiction.   2. Missing persons
    — Fiction.   3. Runaway wives — Fiction.   4. Large type
    books.   I. Title.
    PS3533.U4M87 2003
    813'.52—dc22   2003061342

MURDER
WITH A PAST

CAST OF CHARACTERS

1

Dave Tully reached the outskirts of the business district at five o'clock in the afternoon. Trying to make time, he chose River Street and swung into the car-stream rushing across the bridge. A cloverleaf intersection a mile beyond split the river of traffic into rivulets. The big beige Imperial took the one going east.

Oleander Drive brought Tully in a gentle climb to the short green hills and, a few minutes later, to the fieldstone pillar whose bronze plaque announced Tully Heights.

The stiffness in his legs — it was a long drive up from the state capital — began to leave him. He felt himself smiling.

Tully Heights never failed to relax him. The Heights had been Dave Tully's baby, from the first inking of the plat to the last brad in the graceful ranchers and split-levels slipping past the Imperial.

He had done a very good job here, Tully thought. The street layouts held the secret — broad and meandering, following the natural contours of the hills. At the sacrifice of a few lots he had achieved a beautiful individuality. You came upon each house unexpectedly, as if it were alone in the hills — a miniature estate rather than what it was, a unit in a development.

At number 100 Oleander, Tully braked the big car and eagerly turned into the driveway curving to the double garage doors of a redwood and antique brick split-level.

The absence of the other car, the general air of emptiness, let him down. Still, she hadn't known he would be getting back at this hour.

Tully got out of the car — a big man, big in the shoulders and small in the waist. His face was square-cut, hearty, with a crinkle-eyed glow under the rather surprising metallic gray of his hair. People invariably glanced at the back of his hand for a tattoo, as in the TV cigarette commercials.

Inside the house he called, "Ruth?"

He expected no answer, and he got none.

As Dave Tully's front door swung closed, a sedate black Plymouth sedan rounded the final bend in Oleander Drive. Behind the wheel sat a rangy, thirtyish man who drove with precision. His features were tidy, almost characterless. The late sun glinted on his dark blond, almost tan, hair, which was smoothly trimmed. He wore a dark suit, a white shirt with a short-tab collar and a conservative necktie. The hands on the steering wheel were squarish, with manicured fingernails.

He stopped the Plymouth behind the beige Imperial and got out — nothing hasty in his manner, but not casually, either.

As he passed the Imperial in the driveway he laid his hand, palm flat, on its hood.

The door chimes halted Tully's progress toward the stainless steel kitchen. He wondered if Ruth had forgotten her key. He hadn't thrown the thumb latch on coming in, and the door was locked.

Passing the front windows, Tully glimpsed the black Plymouth and frowned.

He opened the door and said, "Hello, Julian."

The tidy man stepped inside. "Just getting back, Dave?"

"Five minutes ago."

"How'd you make out in the capital?"

"The bond issue looks good. Let's hope the voters pass it when it comes up. And dredging the river seems feasible. Barge shipping would make a city of us in no

13

time at all. How about a sandwich? I drove straight through, and I'm ready to eat raw dog."

"Thanks, I've got beef waiting at home. But don't mind me."

Tully grinned. "Come on into the kitchen. You can mix a drink while I roust a Nature Boy Special out of the refrigerator."

Tully let Julian precede him to the kitchen. He clicked coffee on to heat and went about loading two slices of bread with cold cuts and cheese.

Julian Smith's look bothered him. "You want to explain, Julian?"

"Eat your sandwich," the detective said.

"I get the impression it can't wait." Tully stared at him.

Smith watched a sparrow delouse itself on a twig outside the kitchen window. When the bird fluttered and disappeared, blending into the shadows stealing in from the east side of the house, he said, "As a matter of fact, Dave, it can't."

"Business?"

Smith nodded.

Dave Tully set the sandwich down on the work area beside the sink. "Your department is Homicide, Julian. Somebody get himself killed?"

"Yes."

14

"Well, who?"

"A man named Cranny Cox. The Cranny is short for Crandall."

Tully's broad shoulders loosened, and he laughed. "You had me going there for a second."

"Did I?" the detective said.

"Well, after all. Man hasn't seen his wife in three days and when he gets home there's this character from the mayhem bureau with an official look on his puss." Tully picked up the sandwich and took a man-sized bite.

"The name mean anything to you, Dave?"

"Cranny Cox? Never heard of him. So why the detour on your way home? Of course, we're always glad to have you."

He spoke as if Ruth were standing there in the kitchen with him. Always we, Julian Smith thought. The house had been built for Ruth. Tully was the kind of man who built for the joy of building, and perhaps for that reason he had made a great deal of money out of the Heights. But this house had been a special labor of love.

"Ruth's a little late, isn't she, Dave?"

Tully glanced at the kitchen clock. "She didn't expect me. Probably getting in a positively-the-last rubber of bridge with

15

three other business widows."

"She usually goes on these trips with you, Dave. Why didn't she go this time?"

Dave Tully studied the Homicide man's face with care, and then he set the remains of his sandwich down. "You'd better stop making like a detective, Julian, and tell me what this is all about. In words of one syllable."

Smith reached into a pocket and brought out something wrapped in white cloth. He unwrapped it cautiously. It was a small revolver.

"This is your gun, Dave."

Tully stared and stared at it. "It is?" he said stupidly.

"You bought and registered it when you moved up here."

"Well, sure. You know perfectly well why. This was the first house I finished in the development, and we were pretty much alone up here for a while. I couldn't have Ruth . . ." He stopped and swallowed. He was angry at the policeman, angry at his own dry mouth and panicky thoughts. "For God's sake, Julian! How'd you get hold of my gun? And what's it got to do with this man Cox, whoever he is? What are you trying to tell me?"

"That it killed him," Smith said. "We

fished it out of a sewer near the motel where his body was found."

For some reason Tully found himself groping for the half-eaten sandwich. When he realized what he was doing, he pulled his hand back and gripped the smooth cold edge of the kitchen sink. "What the bloody hell, Julian, are you talking about?"

"I'm sorry, Dave. We've got a pickup on her."

"Pickup on *whom?*"

"Your wife."

"Ruth?" Tully's mouth remained open. "On Ruth?"

"I'm sorry," the detective said again. He pushed away from the window at which he had been standing.

"This is some kind of rib."

"I wish it were, Dave." Smith moved toward the kitchen doorway. "Mind if I look through the house?" He kept moving in the same quiet way without waiting for a reply.

"Look all you want!" Tully shouted after him. "We never even heard of anybody named Crandall Cox! You've just plain flipped, Julian!"

When the detective got to the living room a few minutes later he found Dave Tully standing at the picture window. He had drawn the drapes back as far as they would go, and he was watching the street. His face was a muddier version of his hair.

He turned at Smith's step and asked in a reasonable voice, "Who's this Crandall Cox, Julian?"

"We're not sure yet."

"The gun doesn't mean a damn thing."

"I'm afraid it does, Dave."

"It was just stolen from the house here."

"Did you have a break-in?"

"We must have had."

" 'Must have' isn't admissible evidence. Did you?"

"Not that I know of. But —"

"When is the last time you actually saw this gun?"

"How the devil do I know? A long time ago. Look, Julian." Tully was still sounding reasonable. "I don't get this at all. All right, so somehow somebody got hold of my gun and shot this Cox with it. But why Ruth? You ought to know Ruth couldn't kill anybody."

"How would I know that, Dave?" the detective said. "In fact, how would you know it?"

"Damn you, Julian — !" Tully yelled.

"Keep your shirt on. All I meant was that there's a murder potential in everybody."

"Well, even if she could, why *would* she?

An absolute stranger!"

"Maybe not so absolute." Julian Smith reached into his inside pocket and his manicured fingers reappeared with a police department envelope. From it he very carefully extracted a sheet of notepaper. He unfolded it and laid it on the coffee table. "I'm breaking all the rules, Dave. Read this. Just don't touch it."

Tully came away from the picture window reluctantly. He bent over the table. It was ordinary white typewriter stationery, its creases slightly worn, its message typed. The date in the upper right hand corner suddenly leaped up at him. If it was to be believed, the letter had been written in the short interval between his meeting with Ruth and their marriage:

Cranny —
    You keep away from me, and I mean it. What happened between us is ancient history and you'd better get used to the idea. I've found myself a leading citizen here who's very much interested in me and I think he's going to ask me to marry him. You do anything to spoil my chances and it will be the last thing you *ever* spoil.
    I'm serious, Cranny. Just forget I exist

and go back to your bedroom-window romances and figuring out ways to dodge an outraged bullet. You stand a better chance of surviving at the hands of some dumb cuckold than you do at mine. *I mean this.*

And five weeks from the date on this thing we were married. . . . The notepaper moved a little under Tully's gust of breath. The detective quickly picked it up by two corners, folded it, and tucked it away.

"Typewritten and unsigned," Tully said unsteadily. "What are you trying to pull, Julian? This can't have anything to do with Ruth."

"Maybe," Smith nodded. "But there are other things, Dave. Cox arrived in town four days ago and registered at the Hobby Motel."

Tully knew the place. The hobby for which it was notorious was as old as Adam. The motel skulked on the edge of town, a combination of tavern, restaurant and hot-pillow joint.

"The day after he checked in, Cox went down to City Hall and asked to see a marriage license issued to one Ruth Ainsworth and a man whose name he didn't seem to know. When the news of Cox's murder got

20

out, the license clerk called me from City Hall and told me about Cox's marriage-license hunt.

"Then today . . ."

Tully said thickly, "Well, go on, Julian! What about today?"

"Today a woman who had the room next to Cox's came in to tell us that Cox had himself a party last night. She heard a female voice. And at one point, she says, Cox called the woman he had in his room by name. I'm sorry, Dave, but you'll have to know sooner or later. The name Cox was overheard calling his woman-visitor was Ruth."

Tully walked over to a chair. He sat down, his fingertips clawing at the nubby upholstery. His lips were moving, but nothing came out.

"I want you to take a look at this man, Dave. I hate to ask you to do it . . ."

"It's all right," Tully said. He got up and stood there uncertainly.

Julian Smith took the big man's arm gently. "I wish I could spare you this, Dave. But it's possible Cox isn't his real name. You might recognize him."

2

Smith was deft and quick with the whole thing. A local undertaker handled the town's morgue cases. The man known as Crandall Cox lay under a rubber sheet on a table in the workroom of the Henshaw Funeral Home.

Smith's touch on his arm guided Tully through the heavy sweetness of funeral flowers to the room at the rear. The mortician removed the sheet. Before Tully, in all his naked mortality, lay a stranger.

He was a medium-sized man with little fat bloats around the armpits. The flesh sagged all along the line of his jaw. His face was heavy-featured, almost coarse, with a thin, sporty mustache. The hair was black and wavy and came to a widow's peak on the low forehead. There was one blue-black hole in the gray flab of his neck, just below the thyroid cartilage, like a misplaced third eye.

To Tully the late Crandall Cox looked like nothing human. He tried to visualize Cox with unrelaxed flesh and blood in the tissues of his face, but it was impossible. Even in life he must have looked three-quarters dead — a slug out of some back-alley wall. To think of Ruth — cool, slim, dainty, delectable Ruth — in the arms of this cheap, gray-faced, slop-bodied, slobber-mouthed caricature of a man — made him want to laugh.

Tully looked down at him and thought, You ugly son-of-a-bitch, without any feeling whatever.

"Well?"

Tully turned. "What?" He had forgotten Lieutenant Smith.

"Well, do you recognize him?"

"No."

"You're sure, Dave?"

"Yes."

Somebody opened the door and the flower-smell wriggled in.

"What's the matter?" Julian Smith asked him, eyes on Tully's face.

"It's those damn flowers," he muttered. "Let's get out of here before I throw up."

When they were seated in the unmarked police car, Tully stuck his nose out the window and inhaled.

"Ruth ever mention a man of Cox's description?" the detective asked, starting the car.

"I can answer that one positively absolutely," Tully said without changing expression. "No. How about taking me home, Julian?"

But as they drove off through the gathering darkness, Tully found himself thinking that Ruth had never mentioned much of anything about herself and her life before they had met.

He sat back and shut his eyes. He suddenly felt sleepy.

"Here we are," Smith's voice said.

Tully opened his eyes with a start. They were pulled up behind his Imperial in the driveway of the split-level that had seemed so safe and desirable only an hour ago. The sun had gone down, but the house was dark.

Tully reached for the door-handle.

Smith said, "If you hear from her, Dave, contact me immediately."

Tully looked at him blankly.

"Any other course would be stupid," the Homicide man said. "You realize that, don't you?"

"Yes," Tully said.

"I'll keep Ruth out of the papers as long as possible," the detective said.

"Sure, Julian. Thanks." Tully got out of

24

the car. He was vaguely aware of Smith's hesitation. He shut the door and the detective drove away.

Tully stood still in the middle of the dark yard. He felt very queer — uniquely alone, in a timeless time and a space without margins. Had there ever been a woman named Ruth? Or even a hill, and a house?

Tully shivered and went inside. . . .

He sat in the darkness of his living room going over what Julian Smith had told him on the way to the funeral parlor. The man Cox's body had been found this morning by a Hobby Motel cleaning woman. One of the bathroom towels showed powder burns and multiple bullet holes. The revolver had been wrapped in several folds of the towel to cut down the noise of the shot. He had been shot the night before.

Ruth's face above the towel . . . the tip of her exquisite little nose dead-white, the way it got when she was furious . . .

Tully clutched his temples, but he could not shut out the picture of that imagined motel room, or the voices from his ears.

"Cranny, I told you I never wanted to see you again."

"You won't use that thing, baby. Remember it's li'l ol' Cranny? How's about a drink? Come on, lover, what do you say?"

25

"You promised me, Cranny. You promised."

"So I promised. So what? Here, have a slug of this . . ."

"Stay back! I warned you, Cranny. You shouldn't have followed me. You shouldn't have called."

"You came running, didn't you? You don't fool me, Ruth. You and me always had a thing going for us . . ."

"I came for only one reason — to make you get out of here and leave me and my husband alone!"

"When you've got it made with this sucker and I can cut myself in?"

"No! I won't let you do it. Not to him, Cranny. I love him . . . Stay back, I tell you!"

"Give me that gun —"

It ended there. It always ended there.

Tully leaned back and sighed, feeling a little better.

Ruth indulging in a cheap motel affair for its own sake was simply unthinkable. Especially with a slug like Cox. Yes, even if she had known Cox from somewhere, in the past. Maybe at one time he had been quite different; time and a dissolute life often worked like mold in a damp cellar.

The imaginary dialogue his frantic mind had whipped up could not be too far from the actuality; Tully was sure of it. Cox had been in a position to rake up something about Ruth, something that gave him a hold on her, and she had responded to his motel summons to settle it.

The gun was the giveaway. Ruth would never have taken the gun with her if she had meant to acquiesce in his wishes — obscene, mercenary or otherwise. A woman who intends to climb into bed with an old flame doesn't come to the rendez-vous with her husband's loaded revolver.

It was funny how a thing like that — a conclusion so clear — could make a man's spirits perk, even if the corollary was that his wife had committed murder. First things first, Tully thought wryly.

That long-eared bitch of an eaves-dropper in the next room hadn't heard a bedroom party going on. She wouldn't have been registered at the Hobby in the first place if she was a decent woman. To Hobby habitués any evidence of a couple alone in one of the rooms would mean only one thing.

And another thing. Why, if the woman's ears were so sharp, hadn't she heard the sound of the shot? The towel could hardly have made an effective silencer; there must have been some report. Yet she had not mentioned the shot to Julian. Or having seen Ruth enter — or, more important, leave — Cox's room next door. There was something off-beat in the apparent fact that Julian's witness, a lone woman of prurient curiosity, would overlook the chance to catch a glimpse of the female of the supposed hot-pillow party as she sneaked out of the next motel room. True, the eavesdropper could have had to leave on a date, although no such thing had been mentioned. Or she could have left her room prematurely to cross the motel courtyard to the tavern for a drink, or a pickup.

But, somehow, none of it added up.

Tully felt a small stir, a faint animal warning. That woman would bear investigation . . .

He got up and put on the lights and went to his den and put on the light there. Then he stood over the telephone table and rapidly dialed a number.

"Yes?" It was Norma Hurst's old-woman voice. Norma was not an old woman; the querulous, almost anile, tone was a recent development.

"Norma? Dave Tully."

"Oh," she said. She sounded disappointed. "How was your trip, Dave?"

"All right. Is Ollie there?"

"He's still at the office, and he knows we

have a dinner date, too. . . ." He heard Norma begin to cry.

Through his own preoccupation, Tully felt the old helpless pangs of sympathy. Norma Hurst had been acting oddly for almost a year. The Hursts had had one child, a darling little tow-headed girl with flashing eyes and twinkling legs who was never still. To provide an outlet for her daughter's energies, Norma had bought her a trike. One day the little girl was pedaling wildly down the wrong side of the road when a town garbage truck came around one of Dave Tully's curves and ran over her. The child was killed instantly and horribly. It had taken three men to remove the broken, bloody little body from Norma's arms. Norma could have no other children. She had spent the next five months in a sanitarium.

Tully had never forgotten the day Oliver Hurst had to go to the sanitarium to take his wife home. "Please come with me, Dave," Ollie had begged. "I'm scared to death." "Scared of what, Ollie?" Tully had asked his friend. "They told you Norma's all right now." "The hell they say," Ollie had said bitterly. "I know when Norma's all right and when she isn't. If you ask me, she's never going to be all right — I mean the way she used to be. Dave, I can't get through to her — I don't even know how to talk to her any more. She's always been fond of you. Help me get Norma home." Of course, he had gone. It had been an eerie experience. There had been no outward sign that anything was wrong, but some important ingredient of the old Norma was missing — gone, perhaps forever. Poor Ollie had sat holding her limp hand and chattering away like mad on the trip home. Her only response had been an occasional vague smile.

Tully said into the phone, "Don't upset yourself, Norma. Ollie's undoubtedly on his way home right now, or he'd have called you."

"Why didn't he call me anyway?" Norma wept. "He has no consideration, Dave. I'm so alone all the time — in this awful house —"

"It's one of my best," Tully said fatuously.

"Oh, you know I don't mean that!" To his surprise she stopped crying, sounding angry. "It's just that Ollie keeps avoiding me, and don't tell me he doesn't, Dave Tully!"

"I'll tell you exactly that, Norma. He's the most successful lawyer in town, and he's carrying a tremendous work-load. He spends every minute he possibly can with you."

Norma was silent. For a moment Tully thought she had simply walked away from the phone, as she sometimes did. But then, suddenly, she said, "What did you want Ollie for, Dave?"

It brought Tully back to his own troubles. "Oh, a matter of business, Norma. Would you tell him to give me a ring when he gets home?" He hung up before Norma could ask for Ruth.

Tully sat down at the phone to wait. If ever a man needed legal advice, he thought, it's me right now. Ollie was a damn good lawyer. A little cautious, maybe, but give him time to think a thing through and he was a tough baby to beat.

Tully was still sitting there when he heard somebody moving around in the living room. He jumped up, heart racing. Ruth! Could it possibly be Ruth?

He ran into the living room.

But it was only Sandra Jean.

Sandra Jean was Ruth's sister, and she used her older sister's home as if her name were also Tully, instead of Ainsworth. She was busy at the cowhide-and-bleached mahogany bar when Tully walked in — so absorbed in fixing her Scotch on the rocks that when he said "Hi!" in her ear, she almost dropped the tall glass.

When Sandra Jean saw who it was, she said, "Don't *do* things like that, you creep," giving him one of her characteristic pouty-lipped, moist looks, and turned back to the bar. "You really bugged me, pops. Now I do need one with muscles," and she added a full inch of Scotch to the glass.

"I thought it was Ruth," Tully said. "Do you know where she is?"

"Probably having dinner out," Sandra Jean said, sipping. She gave him a long-lashed, thoughtful look over the rim of her glass. "I guess she didn't expect you home so early. I was kind of working the raised-eyebrow department myself when I saw the car and the lights on — I was just going to look for you when you gave me that verbal goose. But I needed this drink first."

"You're drinking too damned much," Tully said.

"Yes, popsy," Sandra Jean said. "You want to spank the naughty little sister?" She stuck her bottom out at him, laughing.

"Act your age, will you?" Tully sat down wearily.

He wondered only briefly what Sandra Jean was doing there if she had believed he and Ruth weren't home. Ruth's kid sister operated on a sort of emotional radar — "Obey that impulse!" was her motto. She had a key to their house, and if she were in the neighborhood and suddenly felt like a drink, the fact that no one was supposed to be home wouldn't stop her. On the other hand . . .

She was still looking at him over the glass. Tully stirred uncomfortably.

He always had that feeling when he was alone with Sandra Jean. She made him conscious of himself. As if she possessed a secret knowledge, a quivering and un-spoken something between them which shamed him, and amused her. The only thing that made it tolerable was his rueful conviction that Sandra Jean affected most men that way.

She turned from the bar and went over to the TV set and clicked it on, sipping all the time. Tully watched her a little warily. She was an attractive kid, all right. "Kid . . ." Some kid! In many ways she was like Ruth — the same clean-line legs, the same nipped-in waist, flow of hips, full shoul-ders; the same dramatic facial structure, wide-apart eyes, perfect little nose.

Ruth's hair was a sun-drenched auburn and Sandra Jean's was whatever color her frequent whims dictated — right now it was a kind of bangy Cleopatra black — but their real differences were vital, a matter of movement and gesture in carrying out the unconscious commands of their worlds-apart temperaments. If they walked across a room together, observed from either fore or aft Ruth walked like a lady and Sandra Jean like a belly dancer — with the same equipment. There was a smack of sensuality in every move the girl made, almost a naked carnality.

She's going to give some man a hard time, Tully thought dimly. Andy Gordon, if she could wrestle the young nitwit out of mama's clutch. And maybe a procession of others who, like the panting Gordon boy, would mistake Sandra Jean's striptease personality for heaven-sent passion. Tully had long suspected that beneath his young sister-in-law's steamy exterior lay a soul of ice.

The blast of the TV jarred him back to the present. He started to get up, but sank back when Sandra Jean turned the sound down low. She dropped into a chair opposite him, sprawling on the end of her spine, her long legs thrust out as far as they would go. She closed one eye and sighted through the amber liquid in her glass.

"Thought I'd wait around for Ruth and muscle in, if you two are going out tonight," she said. "Lover-boy is dancing attendance on mama and left me at loose ends this evening. You don't mind, do you?"

Tully said nothing. Ruth . . . He shut his eyes and massaged them with the thumb and forefinger of his left hand.

Sandra Jean said suddenly, "Say, what's the matter with you? Trip go sour?"

Tully opened his eyes. "Look, Sandra, don't you have any idea where Ruth is?"

"No. Should I have? You're looking kind of green, Davey. How about a slug of Scotch?"

Tully shook his head and shut his eyes again, wishing she would go away. His temples were pounding. Ruth . . . He tried desperately not to think.

And then a scent insinuated itself into his nostrils, a musky flower-scent that instantly evoked the funeral parlor and the waxworks figure on the mortician's worktable. Tully's eyes flew open. Sandra Jean was stooping over him, careless of the cleft exposed by her low-cut frock, her young breath hot on his face.

"Poor Davey," she moaned, and she stooped lower and put her lips on his surprised mouth, and then she was kissing him hard and thrusting with her tongue.

Something devastating happened to Tully, a reflex of revulsion that made his big hands shoot out and grab the girl's arms and shake her so violently that her head flopped back and forth as if her neck were broken. Sandra Jean yelped softly and dropped her drink; he felt some of the Scotch splash on his trousers. It was the expression on her face, however, that brought Tully to his senses. For a moment she had looked like a terrified child. He shoved her from him and jumped up.

"Don't ever try that on me again, Sandra," he muttered. "Ever, do you understand? Play your erotic games with Andy. I play for keeps." Suddenly he felt ashamed. He turned around and said, "I hope I didn't hurt you."

"But you did." Sandra Jean's moist pout was in evidence again. "You're a brute, do you know that?" She actually wriggled. "Oooh, what a brute. I didn't realize you're so strong, Davey. Shake me again?"

"Oh, shut up," he growled, and walked over to the window. In its reflecting surface he saw the girl staring at his back. Then she shrugged, picked up the remains of the glass, and went off to the kitchen with insolent hips.

The hell with her, Tully thought, staring into the darkness.

Where was Ruth? Why didn't she come home? Or at least call?

Tully set his throbbing forehead against the cool glass. . . .

It was the TV that made him turn around. The early evening newscast had come on, and the newscaster had mentioned the name Crandall Cox.

"Police have made no official statement yet about last night's motel shooting," the man was saying. "But just before air time this reporter learned from an authoritative source that a woman is being sought for questioning, the wife of a prominent local real-estate developer —"

In two strides Tully was at the set, wrenching the dial. The picture and voice faded swiftly.

"So that's it," a voice said behind him.

Tully whirled. It was Sandra Jean with a fresh glass.

"What's it?"

"That's why you're acting so funny. It's Ruth they're looking for, isn't it?"

3

The girl sounded perfectly cool. If she was disturbed, it was more a matter of annoyance than worry. Tully gaped at her.

She went over to the bar and proceeded to fix another drink for herself. "It would have to happen now," she complained.

"Now?" Tully repeated blankly.

"I mean, it's darned inconsiderate of Ruth, getting herself involved in a mess just when I was settling my hooks for keeps in lover-boy. It's certainly not going to help me with old lady Cabbott. She'll snatch at this scandal the way a seal goes after a fish."

"I see," Tully said. He felt like grabbing her by the neck and the seat of the panties and heaving her through the picture window. "And that's all you can think about?"

Sandra Jean sat down again in the same sprawled position and sipped her drink. "Oh, come off it, Davey. It's obviously some kind of ridiculous mistake, and anyway Ruth's always been able to take care of herself. Meanwhile, I have to make out with Mercedes Cabbott. She'll look for any excuse to keep Andy and me apart. My sister being hunted by the police is made to order for that old barracuda."

"I guess this just isn't my day," Tully said. He rubbed his forehead with one hand, leaning on the TV set with the other. "What kind of self-centered little slut are you, Sandra?"

Something very hard came into her eyes. But her voice was quite level as she said, "I don't like that, Davey. Don't call me that again."

"All right, all right," Tully muttered. "I can't seem to grasp any of this, Sandra. Did Ruth know a Crandall Cox?"

"Ask Ruth that," the girl said.

"Then she did!"

"I didn't say that. Look, Davey." Sandra Jean took a long swallow and then set her glass down. "You think I'm being awfully callous, don't you?"

"I think you're being damned unconcerned about a sister who's knocked herself out for you!"

"I'm not unconcerned," the girl said calmly. "It's just that I'm not worried. I know Ruth a lot better than you do."

"What's that supposed to mean?"

"Nothing. Ruth's always managed just fine. She's done pretty well for herself so far, hasn't she? She's never lost her head in her life. She's far too smart to kill anybody, especially a crumb like this Cranny Cox."

Tully straightened up, staring at her. "Crumb? How do you know he was a crumb?"

"He must have been. Who else but crumbs get themselves shot in cheap motels?"

"You're lying," Tully said. "You do know what this is all about, Sandra. You gave yourself away!"

"I did?" she said. She picked up the glass again.

"Cranny. You called him Cranny."

"So what?"

"How do you know he was called Cranny Cox?"

"The announcer called him that."

"The announcer called him Crandall Cox!"

For the merest instant Sandra Jean seemed perturbed. Then she shrugged and sipped her Scotch. "It's obvious, isn't it? A man named Crandall would be called Cranny, wouldn't he?"

"Who was he, Sandra? What was his connection with Ruth?"

The girl rose. "Really, Davey. Playing

detective! You weren't cut out for the role. Good night."

"Not yet!" Tully caught her by the wrist and spun her around. "By God, you know something about this, and you're not leaving here until you tell me!"

"Isn't this where I say, 'Please, you're hurting me'?" she said. "For the second time tonight, I might add. Under other circumstances I'd enjoy it. Now I'm bored. Let go of me."

He glared down at her in a dumb rage. She had a special talent for making him feel foolish. He let go and turned abruptly away.

"You're a darling," his wife's sister said sweetly. "Ruth's lucky to have you. About this Cox business, it's Ruth's show. She's innocent, of course, and I'm perfectly sure she'll clear the whole thing up. Try not to worry about it."

"Will you please get out of here!"

"I'm off to the races right *now*," Sandra Jean said. "Where the devil did I throw my purse? Oh, here it is." He heard her going to the door. "You see, Mercedes Cabbott and that stuffed Adonis she picked for a third husband might decide to pack my beloved off on a long trip, and I've got to get in a few licks of my own or lose Andy for good. How

41

mercenary can a girl get! Night, Davey."

He did not reply, and after a moment he heard the door open and close.

Tully went to the bar and poured himself a long jolt of Scotch. He gulped it and poured himself another. Then he sat down and tried to think again.

Sandra Jean had seemed so positive that Ruth would come through this — whatever it was — in one piece. Of course the girl knew all about it. She must have good reasons for respecting Ruth's confidence.

That was the trouble, Tully thought. Those reasons.

He was completely confused. The implications from some of the things Sandra Jean had said . . . If Julian Smith were to phone him this moment to announce that Ruth was in the clear for Cox's murder, could he honestly say that things would be just as they used to be between them?

He swallowed some more of the Scotch.

What had Cox really been to Ruth? He couldn't have been unknown to her — not when his nickname fell so naturally from her younger sister's lips.

Who *was* Cox?

For that matter, *who was Ruth?*

The question invaded and possessed his mind. . . .

Tully was pouring his third Scotch when the phone in the den rang.

It was Oliver Hurst.

"Ollie," Tully said. He felt a deep gratitude.

"What's up, Dave?" the lawyer's rich voice said. "I just got in and Norma says you sounded upset. Anything wrong?"

"Ollie, can you come right over?"

"Now?"

"Now."

"I don't know, Dave. We've got this dinner engagement, and Norma's all over my back as it is for getting home late."

"Ollie, this won't wait. It's a serious personal matter. Believe me, I wouldn't press it or risk upsetting Norma further if it weren't. I've got to talk to you right away."

Hurst was silent. Then Tully heard him say something, and Norma's voice shrilling in the background. "Dave."

"Yes, Ollie."

"I'll be there in a few minutes."

"Thanks!"

Twenty minutes later Tully saw the lights of Hurst's car swing into the driveway. He hurried to the door.

The lawyer's flesh belied the promise of his voice. He was thick-set and moon-faced, and his head was a freckled, almost hairless, egg. But he had fine, light, clear eyes of a deceptive transparency which sometimes made Tully uncomfortable; they were almost the only remains of the lawyer's youth — it was hard to believe, seeing what he had become, that Ollie had been voted the handsomest man in his class in the college yearbook. His hands were never still — pulling an ear, fingering his chin, rubbing his nose, scratching his skull, pinching the skin of his neck.

But if Oliver Hurst had settled into suet and chronic worry, he also — as Tully knew — had guts. He was a fighter. Back when the town had been little more than an overgrown village dependent on the local college of the state university system, Ollie had bulldogged his way through to a first-class education and a law degree. In those years it had been an exceptional achievement for a day-laborer's son. As the town grew, Ollie had had to make his own opportunities; no one made it easy for him. Until David Tully began to throw business his way. That marked Hurst's break-through; now he handled all Tully's legal affairs, and he was the busiest lawyer in town. He owed a great deal to Dave Tully.

Ollie took a quick look around. "Where's

the fire, Dave? Everything seems normal."

"Drink?"

"You sound as if I'll need it. What's the trouble?"

Tully splashed some bourbon into a glass. "Ruth."

"Ruth?" Hurst looked puzzled. He merely moistened his lips with the bourbon, as if some sixth sense told him he was going to need his faculties unimpaired. "What d'ye mean Ruth? What kind of trouble could Ruth be in?"

"Have you seen her last night or today? Heard from her?"

"No. You mean you don't know where she is?"

"That's right."

Oliver Hurst sat down, staring at the taller man. "It's more than that, Dave. Come on, let's have it."

"She's apparently mixed up in this motel business."

"What motel business?"

Tully was surprised. He had been so preoccupied with the affair that he had assumed it was universally known. "Haven't you heard the newscast, Ollie?"

"No, I just got home. And you know how Norma feels about the news these days — she'll never let me turn the thing on, can't stand the voices of doom." The lawyer rather deliberately set the glass down. "What is this crud about Ruth and a motel, Dave?" he asked quietly.

Tully said in a bleak voice, "And a dead man."

Hurst stared up at him. "And a *what?*"

"A man named Cox. He was shot to death in the Hobby Motel last night sometime — body wasn't found till midmorning."

"So? What's that got to do with Ruth?"

"A gun registered in my name killed him — we kept it in the house here. And a woman in the room next to Cox's says Cox had a gal in his room last night — overheard Cox call her Ruth, she says."

After a moment Ollie Hurst took up the glass of bourbon and drank half its contents. "I see," he said, and he set the glass down again and rose. "How did you learn all this, Dave?"

"Julian Smith told me. He was here looking for Ruth. He has a pickup on her."

"I see," the lawyer said again. He stood frowning, pinching his lips, rubbing his nose, staring at the floor. Finally he looked up. "I don't believe it, Dave. There's something wrong somewhere. It's got to be a mistake."

"That's what I keep telling myself."

"Good God, man, you sound as if you doubt her!"

"Do I?" Tully said.

"Not Ruth, Dave. You ought to know that better than anyone in the world. I can imagine what a shock this is to you, but so-called facts can often be terribly misleading. I'd stake a good deal on Ruth's integrity."

"Then how do you explain those facts?"

"I don't — not yet. But even if Ruth was there last night, there are a dozen possible innocent explanations. Certainly she didn't kill the guy — I can't see Ruth killing a flea, let alone a human being. Who was he, do you know?"

"Who was who?"

"This fellow Cox."

"I haven't any idea," Tully said tiredly. "Julian had me take a look at him over at the funeral parlor. I never saw him before."

Hurst began to walk around the room, deep in thought. "Dave," he said, stopping. "You have no idea where Ruth is? You found no note, no message?"

"No."

"Have you tried calling around?"

"No!" Tully was astounded at the violence of his own tone. "The last thing I want to do is spread this. Julian promised to keep Ruth's name out of the papers as long as he could. It's true somebody leaked a hint to that damn newscaster, but he's still not naming names. Ollie, I thought I knew her, I thought I knew her!"

"You did. You do."

"Do I? How long did I actually know her before we got married? I don't know a thing about her past. She never talked about it. She could have been a call girl somewhere for all I know."

"That's a fine thing to say about your own wife, Dave! I'm surprised at you — I really am."

"Are you?" Tully heard himself shouting. "What the hell would you know about it? Your wife was never reported in a lousy motel room with a creep — your wife never had a murder charge hanging over her head!"

Ollie Hurst said mildly, "Go ahead, take it out on me if it makes you feel any better."

"I don't know what I called you for! Fat lot of help you are!"

"Here, Dave. Drink this."

It was three fingers of Scotch. Tully started to take it mechanically, but then he shook his head. "I've already tried that. I'm sorry, Ollie, I don't know what's happening to me. A couple of hours ago I was living in a solid world, solid business, solid house, in love with a solid wife. All of a sudden everything's turned to jelly — I can't hold *on* to any of it! I don't know what to think, where to turn, what to do . . ."

"You want me to get a lawyer?"

"A lawyer? What do I need a lawyer for? You're a lawyer, aren't you?"

"This is a criminal case. Actually, I don't think you need a criminal lawyer yet, not till Ruth turns up, anyway. But I'll inquire around and have one on tap. The best way I can help right now is to try to locate Ruth. I could ask around discreetly —"

"No," Tully said in a strained voice. "I'm sorry I even dragged you into this. You'd better get back to Norma and that dinner party of yours. She'll be climbing the walls."

"Wait till I finish my drink before you kick me out, will you?" Ollie Hurst said amiably. He sat down and picked up the glass of bourbon. "Look, Dave, I don't pretend to know much about women. I've got my hands full just keeping poor old Norma going. And I certainly don't know anything about Ruth that you don't know. But maybe I can see her more objectively. That wife of yours is something special — and I don't give a damn if she *was* a call girl, which you and I both know she wasn't! The way she's helped Norma, the way she looks at you when she thinks no-body's watching, her honesty and frank-ness and kindness to others. . . . Your wife is a lady, Dave, in the only mean-ingful sense of the word, and if I were to find out different I'd burn my lawbooks and take a job on the county roads. And that's my speech for tonight."

He finished his drink and got to his feet. "Well, I suppose I'll have to tell Norma. Though how I'm going to break the news to her . . ." Hurst sighed and turned to go. "Problems, problems, hey, Dave? But we've got to manage. There's no other choice. Keep in touch, will you? Especially if there's any news about Ruth."

"Good night," Tully muttered.

Was Ollie's judgment right? Except where his own emotions were involved, Ollie knew a lot about women, in spite of his disclaimer. But then why had Sandra Jean insinuated . . . ?

The house, filled with silence, suddenly made itself known to him. Tully found himself looking around, like a child imag-ining monsters in the next room.

He jumped up. He couldn't stay here doing nothing. There was that woman at the Hobby Motel, his feeling that some-thing was wrong with her story. . . .

4

At one time she must have been pink and firm and cheaply pretty, a sexpot joyously ready for a tumble. But the years had caught up with her. Her overblown breasts had grown soft and lifeless, her heavy hips supported a thickening middle, and she was getting jowly. She was wearing a flowered wrapper and curlers in her straw-bleached hair, and there was a patina of cold cream on her fat cheeks when she answered Tully's knock on the motel-room door.

She looked at him impudently. "Yes? What is it?"

"Are you Miss Maudie Blake?"

She nodded.

"My name is David Tully. I'd like to talk to you for a few minutes."

"What about?" She was taking automatic inventory, noting the cut of his clothes, the beige Imperial he had parked nearby. If his surname meant anything to her, he could not detect it.

"May I come in?" Tully asked.

"You a cop?"

"No, Miss Blake."

"A girl never knows," she said, poking at her hair. "You don't look like one. What is this, a sales pitch?"

"I'm not selling anything. I'm the husband of the woman named Ruth."

Her eyes closed to slits.

"I know you've made a statement to the police. You don't have to talk to me, Miss Blake. But I'd appreciate it if you would."

He could see her weighing the possibilities, ready for instant retreat or advance. There was an animal cunning about her. He felt his pulse begin to accelerate. His instinct had been right.

"I guess I got a minute, Mr. Tully. Come in."

She stood aside and he entered the motel room. The air was clogged with heavy perfume and powder. The place was close and hot, like an incubator, and it was cluttered with magazines, newspapers and odds and ends of apparel.

The Blake woman shut the door, waddled to the messy dressing table, picked up a pack of cigarettes and lit one. She did not ask him to sit down, or sit down herself. He waited.

"Mr. Tully," she said suddenly. "You ought to know I can't change my story now."

Tully said to himself, Easy, boy, easy. You've got a bite on your line. "You think that's why I came here?"

She made a vague gesture with her dimpled hands. "Why else? I figured this Ruth babe for a chippie. Now that I see the kind of husband she's got, I get a different picture. Class. A bored dame with everything, including round heels." She clucked, shaking her synthetic locks. "It's too bad. How do broads like that hook guys like you?" The fat blonde cocked her head at him. "Just for laughs, how much were you going to offer me?"

"Miss Blake," Tully began, "I don't think you understand —"

"Only thing is, it's too late." She sighed. "You should have beat the cops here. I'm stuck with what I told them."

"And what you told them was the absolute truth?"

"Sure it was." She looked at him steadily. Too steadily?

"Did you actually see the woman?"

"No. I didn't even know he had a woman in there till I heard her say something. These walls are like tissue paper. After that I listened, just for kicks."

"You heard him call her by name, I understand." He had to hold on to himself with all his strength.

"I sure did."

"How many times?"

"Oh, once or twice."

"Then isn't it possible you made a mistake?"

Her wrapper rustled as she undulated toward him. She came close enough for her various odors to sicken him.

"You're really gone on this wife of yours, ain't you, Mr. Tully? I wish I could say I'm not sure, but how could I make a mistake? He said her name loud and clear."

Tully managed to back off without offending her. Why did I have to come here? he thought.

"You want a drink, Mr. Tully?" the woman asked sympathetically. "You look like you could use one."

"No, thanks."

She shook her head. "What a dope, playing around when she has a husband like you. Have they found her yet?"

"No. I mean I don't know. I don't suppose so."

"Maybe she can explain things when they do."

And maybe she can't. "What time did you hear them in there?" Already it was becoming easier to couple them verbally.

Maudie Blake shrugged, everything jiggling. "Earlier part of the evening. I wasn't watching the time."

"Is there anyone else who might have heard them?"

"I guess not. His room's on the end of the row. No room on the other side."

"And you were able to hear him call the woman by name," Tully said. "How is it you didn't hear the shot?"

"I went out before that, I guess — before she let Cranny have it."

He turned to go, his shoulders at a defeated slope. But then he stopped and turned slowly around.

"Cranny," Tully said. "*You just called him Cranny.* You knew him!" He was all over her in an instant, digging his big fingers deep into her floppy arms, glaring down at her. "In fact, you know a hell of a lot more about this than you've let on! Suppose you start telling the truth —"

"Whoa, buster," the woman said. She had gone a little pale around the edges of the cold cream, but her voice was cool and unperturbed. "I could have you up for assault. Calm down, Mr. Tully. You can bruise me any time you want, but not with that look in your eye. Take your hands off me."

"All *right!*" He almost flung her from him in his frustration. "Then you explain why you called him Cranny."

"I must have heard one of the cops call him that." She actually came close to him again and patted his cheek. "I know, she really gave you the knee. You'll get over it. You in the phone book?"

"What?" Tully said, trying to shake his head clear.

"I said you in the phone book."

"Of course. Why?"

"I thought you might have an unlisted number — you look well-heeled enough."

"Why did you ask?"

"Oh, so I could get in touch. In case I thought of something. . . . No, I can't right now," she added hastily, seeing his expression. "But you know how it is. Sometimes a person remembers . . . later."

Tully said tiredly, "Maybe Lieutenant Smith could jog your memory right now, Miss Blake."

"I doubt it," Maudie Blake said, smiling. "I'd just have to tell him the same thing over and over. But I like you, Mr. Tully. And I'm going to set my mind to work real hard to see if I can think of anything else."

Tully stood beside the Imperial immobilized between despair and hope. Some of the Blake woman's statements had had a horribly truthful ring. And yet . . . He kept shaking his head.

After a while he trudged across the parking strip to the office of the motel. Behind the desk was the dried-up old cutthroat who had given him Maudie Blake's room number. The old man was reading the evening *Call*.

"What's it this time?" he grunted, not looking up.

"Sorry to bother you again," Tully said. "But I'd like to know when Miss Blake checked in."

"You would, would you?"

"Yes." Tully began to feel the rumble of anger again. A little more of this and I'll blow like a volcano, he thought.

"Can't give out information 'bout our guests."

"A dollar bought me her room number." Tully fished in his wallet and flung two dollar bills on the desk. "When did she check in?"

The old man lowered his newspaper, looked around cautiously, and clawed the two bills out of sight. "Look, mister," he said in a low voice, "this place has been crawlin' with cops. They told me to keep my trap shut. I'll do it this one more time, but that's it." He scuttled over to a card file and went through it fast. "The tenth. That would be four days ago. Now beat it, mister, will you?"

"Thanks," Tully said grimly.

He went out. There was a ferment of exultancy in him now. Maudie Blake had checked in four days ago. The same day as Cox! Surely . . . ? He thought of the Witch in *Macbeth*. "By the pricking of my thumbs . . ." Was it likely that Julian Smith, with all his experience, hadn't seen a possible connection between the Blake woman and the dead man?

The exultancy drained out of him.

Tully plodded over to his car, carefully not looking at the end room of the row. One look on his arrival had been plenty. It was too easy to imagine Ruth stealing up to it, glancing around, knocking surreptitiously. . . .

He drove home in a torment of doubt.

How could a man live in love with a woman and not *know* her? Was Ruth capable of putting on an act that had fooled not only him, but his friends as well? Including a shrewd observer like Ollie Hurst?

It's ridiculous and unreasonable, Tully kept telling himself. The actress didn't live who could carry off such a role for so long.

Ruth had travelled widely. She had finished her education abroad and had a rather cosmopolitan outlook. So she was not particularly interested in the petty social cliques of a small town. She had been quite frank — with him — about her views on living there. But she hadn't minded the smallness so long as she lived there with him, and nobody but him was aware of her attitude. She joined into the life of his set happily, if on her own terms. Practically everyone was crazy about her.

You couldn't paint that sort of honesty into a picture of an adulterous killer.

Or could you?

His doubts were less insistent as he got out of the Imperial in his driveway. The house was still dark. He made a quick, futile search anyway. Then, because he could no longer resist, he began telephoning friends. He explained that he had returned from the capital sooner than he had expected. Was Ruth there?

He received invitations to golf, a dinner, a bridge session, but no clue to his wife's whereabouts. If any of them had heard of the Crandall Cox murder, none had yet connected Ruth with it.

Between calls to others, he kept trying

Mercedes Cabbott's number. It continued busy. As he was about to try it for the fourth time, someone rang the doorbell.

Ruth?

But it was only Mercedes Cabbott's son, Andrew Gordon.

Andy wore his usual sulky look. His breath was rich with liquor.

"I was just trying to get your mother, Andy —"

The son of Mercedes Cabbott's second marriage brushed by Tully. He was a dark, lean, sullenly good-looking boy who might have been handsome if his features had had any strength. Tully suddenly realized that Andrew Gordon had a habit of pouting, uncomfortably like Sandra Jean Ainsworth. Too bad his character wasn't as muscular as his body.

"Is Ruth at your place, by any chance?" There was no point in challenging Andy's rudeness. He had been brought up in an atmosphere of special privilege.

"Nah," Andy said. "Where's Sandra Jean?"

"I don't know."

"She said she was stopping by here to kill a loose evening."

"She did. Then she left to look for you."

"Damn," Andy said. "Well, it looks as if neither of us is having any luck with the Ainsworth sisters tonight. Got a drink handy?"

"You know where it is."

But Tully noticed that Andy went heavy on the water and light on the Scotch. He always acted tighter than he was.

Andy clutched the drink and threw his leg over the arm of a chair.

"I had a real brawl with the old lady," Andy said. "I was supposed to squire her around this evening, but then we got into it. It's that damned George's fault. Can't Mercedes see he married her for the loot?"

Tully knew the petulant statement to be false. George Cabbott, Mercedes's third husband, was a little younger than she, but he had plenty of money of his own. George was a husky, no-nonsense fellow who didn't care a hoot what people thought of him. He wasn't afraid of hard work, public opinion, or anything else. He and Mercedes were genuinely attached to each other, a fact nobody but Tully and a few other perceptive people believed.

"One of these days," Andy promised, "I'm going to push George's nose through the back of his neck."

It might be a pretty good brawl at that,

Tully thought. Physically Andrew was gristle, bone and cat-gut. George was a hundred and eighty pounds of rock-crusher.

"I could handle the old lady and marry Sandra Jean," Andy continued to mutter, "if George would keep his nose to himself. He's got my respected mother so worked up against Sandra Jean the old lady'll use any excuse to break us up."

Such as a sister hunted for murder? Tully wondered, and then winced at the absurdity of it.

Andy held his glass up to the light, squinting. To hide the misery? Tully felt sorry for him at that. The boy had had it pretty rough.

In her globe-trotting, gadabout career Mercedes had picked up a string of husbands. By two of these she had borne children. Her daughter Kathleen's father had been a man named Lavery. Andrew was the offspring of Lavery's successor, a mining tycoon named Gordon. Andy had been a small boy when his half-sister, already a young woman, died in a boating accident. This had been fifteen years ago.

In her daughter's grave Mercedes had buried her maternal common sense. She had never worn an apron in her life, but the strings by which she tied her son to her

had been no less hampering. She had pro-
tected Andy from everything, including his
opportunity to become a man.

"Maybe Sandra Jean ran into Ruth,"
Andy said. "They'll probably come home
together."

"I don't think so," Tully said. "I don't
think there's any point in waiting, Andy."

Andy's lip twitched. "Is that a gentle hint
to leave?"

"No," Tully said. "Though if you're going
to get argumentative, it might be a good
idea."

"Everybody, but everybody!" Andy exploded. He looked as if he wanted to throw
the glass. "Like a stinking conspiracy. Send
Andrew home so mama can tuck him into
his itty-bitty bedikins! I'm getting so
damned fed up —"

"Look, kid," Tully said, "I've got too
much on my own mind tonight to listen to
your bellyaching."

"You? What kind of trouble could the
noble Dave Tully be in?"

"Skip it."

"First you insult me, then you tell me to
skip it! You trying to make me out a
nothing?"

"You do a pretty good job of that yourself, Andy."

"You'd better apologize for that," the boy said excitedly. "I'm not going to stand for that —"

"All right, I apologize," Tully said wearily. "Now will you start acting your age?"

"You stop talking to me as if I were still wearing diapers!"

"Well, aren't you? Andy, I've asked you to lay off me tonight. Ruth is in the worst kind of trouble. Some man has been killed in the Hobby Motel and, unbelievable as it is, the police think she killed him. They're looking for her now."

Andrew Gordon's skin underwent a remarkable series of color changes, from its normal sun-brown through a number of gradations of mud-tan to a final, dirty yellow. There it remained. The boy stared up at Tully as if he had received a fatal wound. Slowly he got to his feet.

"Ruth? Wanted for *murder?"*

"I told you it was unbelievable."

Mercedes Cabbott's son moistened his lips. "She wouldn't do that to me and Sandra Jean — she couldn't —"

"What?" Tully said, bewildered.

"I always thought that angel-puss of Ruth's was too good to be true," the boy mumbled. "I tagged her for a cheap lay long ago. But to kill the guy and drag

64

Sandra Jean into the papers just when . . . Sure as hell, this is going to blow it with the old lady —"

Andy staggered backward across half the room, landing with a jarring impact against the wall, his hand to the cheek on which Tully's heavy fist had landed.

"Say anything like that about Ruth again and I'll tear that filthy tongue of yours out by the roots."

Tully stood rigid, fighting the steel band tightening about his chest. He kept watching the boy murderously, licking his torn knuckles.

Andy Gordon lurched away from the wall. There was a wild look in his eyes, a sort of crazed happiness.

Tully set himself for a brawl.

It failed to come. Instead, the boy grinned. "So I'm wrong about Ruth, huh? Man, you're as blind as they make 'em."

"I wasn't kidding, Andy. You'd better get out of here now."

"You'd rather not hear it, huh?"

In spite of himself, Tully growled, "Hear what?"

"While you were away upstate, she had a man calling her here. And he wasn't anybody in our crowd, either."

"You're lying," Tully said. "Or making

something out of nothing."

"Am I?" Andy Gordon laughed. "Let me ask you one question. I know the answer because I heard the newscast, but I don't know if you did. What was the name of the guy they found shot in the Hobby?"

"Crandall Cox."

"So you do know. Good enough! Now you listen to me, big man, because I'm going to give it to you good, where it's going to hurt the most." The young voice crackled with hate. "I was out for a drive with Sandra Jean a couple days ago when she said, 'Let's drop in on my sister and cheer the poor darlin' up.' So we dropped in. Your poor darlin' wasn't home. We helped ourselves to some of your liquor, and just then the phone rang. Sandra Jean told me to answer it, so I did. It was a man with a funny kind of voice — flat and sneery and like he talked out of the side of his mouth. A voice I never heard. He asked for Ruth — he didn't say Mrs. Tully, Dave-boy, he used her first name. I said she wasn't here and asked if he wanted to leave a message. He said, 'I sure do,' and the way he said it — well, 'drooly' would be the only word to describe it. And then he said, 'Tell Ruth that Cranny called,' and he hung up. Crandall Cox — Cranny; get it, Mr. Tully? Do you get it?"

Tully rubbed his eyes. He had an over-whelming wish to lie down and go to sleep and sleep on and on and on.

"Did you tell Sandra about the call?" Tully said.

"Why, sure," Andy Gordon said gayly. "No secrets between *us*. But don't worry, Dave, it's all in the family. *We* won't tell anybody. . . . Say, you throw a pretty good punch, do you know?"

And, still grinning, the boy left.

5

Julian Smith's office at police headquarters was as tidy as Smith himself. He nodded pleasantly to Tully and indicated a chair.

"Don't bother to ask, Dave," the lieutenant said. "The answer is we still haven't found a trace of her."

Tully sank into the chair. "When you phoned me to come right over, Julian, I was hoping —" Tully stopped without hope.

Smith filled two paper cups from a container of coffee and offered one to Tully.

"She hasn't tried to contact you, Dave?"

He shook his head.

The lieutenant regarded him with sympathy. "Not much sleep last night, I take it."

"Not much."

"You look as if you could use some lunch."

"I'm not hungry. Julian, why'd you call me?"

"We have a rundown on Crandall Cox."

Tully set the paper down on the Homicide man's desk; it was scalding his hand.

68

He felt as if he weighed a thousand pounds. The headache still drummed between his temples.

"Have you linked Ruth to him?"

The detective said, "Not yet."

"I told you," Tully said. "It's some nightmarish mistake." Where was she? Running? Hiding?

Julian Smith glanced at him again, then picked up some papers from his desk. You'll be interested to learn that Cox originally came from these parts."

"Really?" It was just something to say.

"As a matter of fact, the name Cox rang a bell the minute I heard it. This fellow's father, Crandall Cox Senior, owned a big hardware store where the Macklin department store now stands. He — the father, I mean — served a couple of terms on the City Council."

"I don't remember him."

"It was a long time ago. Junior was the apple of his father's eye — a rotten apple, as it turned out. Kicked out of school — he went to college here — wouldn't go into the business, thought the world owed him a living; you know the type. When Cox Senior died and the store was sold, Junior ran through the estate in short order. Spent it mostly on women. Then his mother died.

He had no other family here, so Cox liquidated what was left and lit out for bigger fields.

"Through his fingerprints, clothing labels, baggage and a few other leads we got a quick make on him from upstate and a few big cities in neighboring states. He was arrested and tried at least twice for extortion, once on a charge of blackmail, but no convictions." Lieutenant Smith shrugged. "There's probably a big book on him that'll turn up when we've had more time to dig."

"Sounds charming," Tully said dully.

"Until comparatively recently Cox lived pretty well. Off women. Mainly middle-aged widows and well-heeled married women with busy husbands and too much time on their hands."

Tully flushed at that, and Smith went on, looking through his window at the town's main street. "About a year or so ago he began to go to pot physically — kidneys kicked up, an almost fatal pneumonia, a stomach ulcer, heart attack. . . . He wound up in the charity ward of a city hospital, and we're pretty sure he headed for here not long after he was discharged.

"Dave . . . I don't think Cox came back to the old home town for sentimental reasons.

He was sick and broke, and the way I figure it he had a pigeon here ready to pluck — some woman he could blackmail out of a lot of money. And she lost her head and killed him."

"You mean Ruth," Tully said.

"The shoe seems to fit, Dave."

Tully swallowed the dregs of his coffee, crushed the paper cup and flung it at the window. Smith patiently picked it up, dropped it into his wastebasket and waited.

Tully's skin was gray and his eyes looked as if they had been wiped with sandpaper.

"Thanks for nothing!" he said through his teeth.

"It may not be so bad, Dave. She'd certainly get the sympathy of a jury. Probably could even plead self-defense and get away with it. Why don't you think it over?"

Tully laughed. "You think I'm hiding Ruth?"

"You're head over heels gone on her, pal. It might have warped your better judgment."

"This is one nightmare that seems to have no end." Tully's laugh was more like a bark. "What good would it do me to hide her, Julian?"

"You might be figuring on smuggling her out of the country — Mexico, South America, anywhere. Then turning your assets secretly into cash and slipping away to join her."

"Julian, you can't be serious —"

"Can't I?" the detective said. "Item: We're pretty good at looking for people. Ruth's hiding in no back-street hotel in this town, believe me. Item: You cut short your visit upstate. Why, Dave?"

"I'd finished sooner than I'd expected. I'd only just got back to the house when you drove up and found me!"

"Or you left the capital two hours before you claimed. Figuring normal driving time, there's still about two hours of your return trip we can't account for, Dave. Maybe more, if you really pushed the Imperial."

"You mean," Tully snarled, "I'm a suspect in this case, too?"

"Under the circumstances," Lieutenant Smith said unhappily, "I'm afraid I've got to ask you what you did with those two hours."

Tully drew the back of his hand across his mouth, tasting a clammy slick. It had not occurred to him that he might be under investigation, too.

"For one thing, I got a shave and haircut," he said.

"At the Capitol Hotel barber shop?"

"No, at a place near Monument Square.

Not far from the restaurant where I had my breakfast."

Smith reached for a scratch pad and a pencil. "Want to give me the name of the shop?"

"I don't know the name of the shop. I don't remember what the barber looked like, or the shine boy. I didn't realize I'd need them for an alibi or I'd have taken notes, Julian."

"You didn't spend two hours in the shop," the Homicide man said. His face was slightly flushed.

"Of course not! I decided that as long as I was in the capital, I'd take a quick look at the Markham development. The one with the artificial lakes."

"Did you call Mr. Markham?"

"No. He'd have insisted on showing me everything in detail and I'd have lost half a day. I was only interested in his use of the terrain. I drove out there, cruised around, saw what I wanted to see, and then left."

"You drove directly home from there?"

"Yes."

"Okay, Tully, thanks."

Tully drove away from police headquarters depressingly certain that Julian Smith was far from through with him.

It was easy enough to see it from the

detective's point of view: Tully returning early from upstate; Ruth, skulking in a darkened house, waiting for her husband, half out of her mind, hysterically confessing in his arms that she had shot a blackmailer; Tully, completely in love with his wife, hiding her without thought of the consequences . . .

Bleakly, he almost wished it were that simple.

6

The mansion — no one ever referred to it as a house — lorded it over the landscape from its eminence above the town. It was a gigantic white-brick edifice with the tall white pillars and sweeping verandas of the Virginia Colonial style, out of place and out of time. But if you could ignore the modern developments clustering about its skirts, and the grimy town far below, it was beautiful.

Tully drove up the winding approach between the immaculate palisades of seventy-foot arborvitae trees, worth a fortune in themselves, catching glimpses of the intricate terracing beyond that kept a crew of landscape gardeners busy nine months a year. Then he passed the tennis courts and the Olympic-sized swimming pool. Over the hill behind the house, Tully knew, were stables and riding trails and a nine-hole golf course, separated from the rear terrace by an immense acreage as carefully tended as a Londoner's postage-stamp garden.

The English butler — only Mercedes Cabbott would have the nerve to employ an English butler in a community where the acquisition of a cook or even a mere maid was a major triumph — preceded Tully through the gleaming two-story entrance hall and showed him out onto the flagged terrace at the rear of the mansion, overlooking the incredible lawns. Mercedes was seated in flowered grandeur at a white-ribbed glass table, big enough for twelve, before a display of savory-smelling silver-lidded mysteries.

"Good morrow, David," she said.

"Good what?" Tully said, in spite of himself.

"What else can I call it? I don't know whether the hell it's morning or afternoon — whether this is breakfast Edouarde whipped up for me, or lunch. What is it, Stellers?"

The butler said, dead-pan, "A bit of each, Madam."

"Thank you, Stellers. How about disposing of this grapefruit for me, David? It's laced with sherry. Or would you care for some he-man chow?"

"I only dropped in for a few minutes, Mercedes —" Tully began.

"And a great mercy it is, David — you look half starved. Pull up one of these spidery iron chairs George picked — I can't imagine why! Another place, Stellers, and tell Edouarde to fix Mr. Tully a filet. Medium rare, David, isn't it?"

Tully smiled faintly. "That's right. But really —"

"Shut up, darling. It will make me happy. Don't you want to make me happy?"

Sipping Edouarde's Lucullan coffee, listening to Mercedes Cabbott's brisk small-talk, Tully resigned himself to a long session. She was a tinkling, vivacious little woman, all pinks and whites, with the figure of a young girl and the temperament of a fifteenth century queen. She wore her white hair like a crown and left the dye bottles to commoner females.

No one told Mercedes what to do, not even her husband George Cabbott, whom she adored. She kept whimsical hours, ate when she pleased, abhorred exercise and never gained a pound. She was a many-sided creature with unpredictable moods, and the inherited millions to indulge them. She would suddenly take off for Europe, or India, or some unannounced destination and be gone for months. She would often, without explanation, refuse to support a much-needed community project; yet Tully knew that she just as often made huge anonymous donations to causes or institutions that caught her fancy.

This youthful woman with the imperious blue eyes was old enough to be a grandmother many times over — which she would have been, she had once remarked to him, had her daughter Kathleen Lavery lived. Tully knew how much Mercedes wanted grandchildren — grandchildren of "the right sort." He supposed this had something to do with her ferocious possessiveness toward Andrew Gordon, her only remaining child, and the fierce eye she kept on the girls in whom he showed an interest.

Tully had known Mercedes all his life as most others in town had known her, which was to say not at all. Then his plans to build Tully Heights brought them together. During their negotiations for the purchase of the land he wanted for his development, they had become friends.

It was through Mercedes Cabbott that he had met Ruth Ainsworth. Ruth had exploded into Tully's life when she made a sudden appearance in the storybook mansion as Mercedes's house guest that memorable summer. Mercedes's insistence on making the wedding for them had seemed to touch Ruth deeply; Tully, who had other plans, found himself abandoning them without a struggle.

It was at the wedding that he first met his bride's sister; Sandra Jean had come from somewhere in the East to be Ruth's maid of honor. And in the mansion Sandra Jean had remained, playing a rapidly warming game with Andy Gordon, as a sort of quasi-member of the family. The Ainsworth girls' mother and Mercedes had been intimate friends since their college days, it seemed, and Mercedes had characteristically kept an eye — and often a hand — on her friend's daughters when Mrs. Ainsworth died. Between Mercedes and Ruth there had been an obvious affection; toward Sandra Jean the wealthy woman evinced no such personal involvement. Their relationship was too complex for Tully to grasp.

He had once asked Mercedes, "Sandra Jean seems to bring out the iron in you. Why do you let her stay?"

"Because," Andy's mother had replied sweetly, "here I can keep tabs on what she's up to."

Something Mercedes was saying jolted Tully out of his ruminations.

"Sorry," he said. "I was off on Cloud Nine. What was that again, Mercedes?"

"I said you're not eating your steak. Now let's talk turkey. When are you going to get down to the reason for this visit? I know it's about Ruth."

Tully put down his steak-knife. "How did you know?"

"Darling, two men were here. Policemen. Very discreet and well-mannered. And pathetically anxious to sniff out Ruth's whereabouts."

"Did you tell them?" Tully asked quickly. "Do you know?"

"No, David, to both questions."

"She's in serious trouble," he muttered.

"I gathered as much," she said in a quiet voice. "David, what's it all about? Tell me, please."

"She's suspected of causing a man's death. His name was Crandall Cox."

"That motel shooting?" The little woman had guts of steel. Her eyes turned steely, too. "We shan't let them harm her, shall we, David?"

"Not if I can help it."

"Not if *we* can help it." Mercedes glanced over her shoulders into the house. "I wonder what's keeping George?"

"Mercedes . . . have you heard from Ruth?"

She returned her attention fully to him. "I'm not sure I'd tell you even if I had."

"What do you mean!"

Mercedes Cabbott leaned over and squeezed his big hand with her tiny one; it had surprising strength. "You needn't bark at me, David," she said gently. "You'd have a troubled look of a different sort if your concern were without a doubt. There's a big question in your mind suddenly about Ruth."

"I don't know what you mean," Tully said stiffly.

"You know exactly what I mean. It's Ruth's possible relationship with this worm Cox that's eating away at you, not the absurd allegation that she shot him."

"Well, suppose it is!"

"Then I was right. I don't blame you one little bit, David. It's natural for a man to doubt under such circumstances."

"Is it?" Tully said miserably. "I always thought that if a man loved a woman —"

"Garbage! A man is a man, which means that he's a peculiarly vulnerable creature." Mercedes smiled at him. "But I have good news for you, David. Natural as your doubts are, they're unnecessary. I know Ruth through and through. She really loves you. No other man exists for her —"

"Would you make the same statement in the past tense?" he mumbled. "A man, say, named Cox?"

"Do you think you have a right to expect that Ruth was brought up in a bottle?" She squeezed his hand again. "But I'd stake a very great deal on that girl, David. I've never known her to do a vulgar or sordid thing."

Tully sighed. "I'm sorry, Mercedes."

"That's good." The blue steel came back into her eyes. "Because now I can say I'm sorry, too."

He looked up, puzzled. "You? What for?"

"For what I have to do, David. I have to use what weapons fate puts into my hand."

"I don't think I understand."

"In a short time you and Ruth are going to be hip-deep in the worst slops of a sex and murder scandal. I mean publicly. I'm going to have to use it, David."

"That's just what Sandra Jean predicted."

"She did?" Mercedes nodded. "Good for her — she's even shrewder than I gave her credit for. Funny how an angel like Ruth could have such a little bitch of a sister. A bitch, I might add, in continuous heat."

Tully said, without thinking, "It takes two to couple, Mercedes."

For a moment she looked furious. Then she shrugged her pretty shoulders. "Yes, it does, David. I suppose you're justified in taking that tone about Andrew — I haven't always sounded rational about my son. I'm afraid I haven't done a very good job with Andy." Her voice hardened. "But he's all I have left, and he's going to be what I want in spite of himself.

"When I buried Kathleen . . ." Mercedes stopped; for the merest flash of a startling instant, she looked ancient. All Tully could think of was Rider Haggard's Ayesha swiftly crumbling to dust. Then Mercedes was herself again. "I wasn't able to stop mourning Kathleen, David. And when I was left with Andy Junior, the ghost of Kathleen took over. What I mean is . . . I was terrified from that moment on. Terrified that I might lose him, too."

He had never seen Mercedes Cabbott so nakedly distressed.

"I've become increasingly aware of the poor job I've done with Andy. Maybe it was marrying George Cabbott that opened my eyes. Third time the charm, they say. George is the man I should have met and married in the beginning. If he'd been at my side in Andy's formative years, to help me bring Andy up . . ."

"Mercedes."

"No, let me say it, David. I want you to know . . . I honestly don't feel any personal spite toward Sandra Jean. Under other circumstances, in fact, I could like the girl — she's so like me in so many ways. But it's too late all around. Andy is what I've made him, a useless and overprotected lunkhead who doesn't know how to take care of himself. He wouldn't survive six months outside the environment I've created for him. But finally knowing all this doesn't change anything. I love him, and I've got to keep him from coming to serious harm. Sandra Jean would swallow him like a female shark. . . . Have I been awfully selfish, filling your ears with my true confessions when you're in such immediate trouble? Forgive me, David."

"For what?" Tully said. He engulfed her little hand and felt it stiffen in his grasp. She was an island surrounded by an impenetrable reef — a strange and lovely little island full of unexpected hazards. No one, with the possible exception of George Cabbott, had ever really explored her.

At that moment George Cabbott came out on the terrace, and Tully rose, feeling a great relief.

George was a big man, as big as Tully, bronzed and bleached by outdoor living. He wore old jeans, a T-shirt and sneakers as if they were a uniform.

" 'Lo, Dave. Sorry I'm late, sweetheart. I was scrubbing up."

As her husband stooped to kiss her, Mercedes crinkled her little nose.

"You've been in the stables again, darling. Sometimes I think I married a horse."

George Cabbott chuckled, and she threw her head back for his kiss. Tully looked away and took the first opportunity to excuse himself.

He had never felt so alone in his life.

Pulling into his driveway, Tully thought he would burst from the pressures building up inside him. He was tired of waiting for Julian Smith to locate Ruth; he had to do something on his own.

And a new fear was gnawing away at him. Was Ruth's continued absence really voluntary? It was possible that she had seen something at the Hobby Motel that had made her a danger to someone. Maybe the police couldn't find her because her body. . . .

Tully ground his teeth and tried to shut out the thought. . . .

Inside the house something was different.

Tully stood holding his breath, trying to sense what it was.

Then he had it. The silence — the silence was gone. With a hoarse cry he made for the master bedroom.

Someone was taking a shower.

He flung himself at the bathroom door.

"Ruth!" he shouted. "Is that you?"

"It's me, Davey — Sandra Jean."

Tully stood there. Finally, he walked out.

He was in the living room when Sandra Jean joined him, her skin warmly moist where it showed beneath the short terrycloth robe. Ruth's robe, damn her! She padded to him, bare legs glistening. Her face was scrubbed shiny, her hair fell in damp ringlets on her forehead. She reminded him so much of Ruth that he had to turn away.

"Mind if I borrow a dress from Ruth, Davey?"

He could have throttled her. He controlled himself. "Help yourself."

"And a cigarette from you?"

He fumbled in his jacket pocket. She stood close to him, as he lit it for her. Damn her soul, did she have to smell like Ruth, too?

She looked up at him slowly. "Thank you, pops."

She had scarcely bothered to draw the robe together.

"Mmm," she said, inhaling deeply. "This tastes good. Change your brand, Davey?" She laughed, and somehow the robe came apart.

"Sandra Jean," he said softly.

She tilted her head. "Yes?" An amused light danced in her eyes.

"Why the hell," he said in the same soft tone, "don't you go and get dressed?"

The light in her eyes shifted to the other end of the spectrum. She wrapped the robe about her tightly and stamped out of the room.

When she reappeared she was wearing one of Ruth's print dresses and a pair of Ruth's flat-heeled straw shoes. Her glance at Tully was spiteful. She went to the bar and mixed herself a drink.

Tully dropped into a chair. "Waiting for someone?"

"Do you mind, Mr. Tully?"

"I'm not sure I don't. Andy, of course?"

"Of course."

"I should think my house would have lost its charm for him as a trysting place."

"Trysting place!" The girl laughed. "You *are* from Squaresville, aren't you?"

"Strictly," Tully said. "But, Sandra, let's keep our eye on the ball, shall we? I don't know what Andy's version was, but last time he was here he made a couple of unpardonable remarks about Ruth. Viciously nasty."

"And you popped him one," Sandra Jean jeered. "But we understand, Davey. You were under a great strain, and all that jazz."

"I still am."

"Andy forgives you. I forgive you. Do you forgive you?"

"I'm sorry I blew my top. But he had it coming."

"Going, as I heard it." Sandra Jean took a thirsty swallow. "You don't care a lot for my fella, do you?"

"I couldn't care less. I wish you'd meet him somewhere else."

"Like in a dirty room in a dirty motel . . . like?"

Mercedes Cabbott is dead right, he thought. This kid is a bitch. "I suppose that's a sisterly reference to Ruth."

"Is *that* what it was?" Sandra Jean asked innocently. "Who's being the nasty little boy now?"

Tully shrugged. He was too exhausted to reply.

Hips on gimbals, Sandra Jean prowled about the room, gesturing with her glass. "You get one thing straight, O Pure in Heart. Nobody wrecks me with Andy, but *nobody*. Mercedes Cabbott can maneuver herself dizzy, you can bar me from this house, but that thar gold strike's mine! Get me?"

"Not that I give a damn," Tully murmured. "But it isn't as if you were penniless."

"Those icky little trust funds Ruth and I inherited? They might look like a ten-strike to a girl who had to pull herself up by the runs in her stockings, but it's strictly for the *hoi polloi*, buster. I need as much in a month as that fund brings me in a year.

Something in the way she said it sounded an alert. But he kept his own voice casual.

"You wouldn't be in a financial jam, would you, Sandra?"

"Oh, I owe a few people." She said it indifferently, but he noticed a slight frown.

It came to him in a flash. "Gamblers, maybe?"

"It's none of your business," she said, and he knew he was right. There were several gambling joints just outside the town limits, and Sandra Jean liked to play the wheel. "Anyhow, it hasn't a thing to do with my greedy plans involving Andrew. He's the biggest chance I'll ever get, and I'm not letting him get away from me. You remember that, sweetie."

The door chimed.

Sandra Jean looked at her brother-in-law. "That's my Andy now," she said, "and if you've any idea of telling him what I just said, forget it. In the first place he wouldn't believe it. In the second place, I can get pretty nasty myself, Sir David."

Tully said dryly, "I never had the least doubt of it," and he got up and opened the door.

George Cabbott stood there.

"Oh, George," Tully said.

"Anything new on Ruth?" The big bronzed man had changed from jeans and T-shirt to a conservative suit.

"No."

"If she'd met with any harm, Dave, you'd have heard by this time. By the way, is Sandra Jean here?"

"Here I am," Sandra Jean said. She was standing stock-still in the middle of the living room. "Hi, George. Is something wrong?"

Cabbott said pleasantly, "That would depend on the point of view. I dropped by to tell you you needn't wait for Andy to show up — if, of course, that's what you're doing here."

"I don't think I understand."

"He's having a long, long talk with Mercedes."

"Oh, one of those." Sandra Jean laughed, but Tully noticed that her eyes remained wary.

"I don't think this one is *quite* like the others," Cabbott said. "I'm afraid Mercedes has pretty well made up her mind to cut Junior off without a cent, as the saying goes, in a certain contingency."

"How does that involve me?" the girl said. "Or is that the whole point?"

"Judge for yourself, Sandra," George Cabbott said, and Tully could have sworn there was an undertone of amusement in his voice. "The last thing I heard Mercedes tell Andy as I left was that, in her opinion, if he was old enough to take a wife he was old enough to get a job and support her."

"Now, George," Sandra Jean said, and there was amusement in her voice, too. She can sure put on an act, Tully thought. She's about as amused as a lady spider watching her dinner get away.

George Cabbott merely smiled and left.

7

"If that refugee from a TV commercial thinks he can bluff me out of this . . . !" Sandra Jean was raging up and down the room. "I'll show *him.*"

"Maybe he's being your very good friend," Tully said.

"And maybe Mercedes Cabbott is a member of the human race! Why, Dave, she put him up to this — isn't it obvious? I'll show her, too!"

There was a bubble of froth at the corner of her mouth. And her sister's predicament, Tully thought bitterly, left her temperature unchanged. That's what she thinks of Ruth.

As if she had picked up the name on her emotional radar, Sandra Jean said suddenly, "I'm not really worried — that woman won't cast her precious sonny-boy adrift — it's the way she treats *me.* You'd think I was Typhoid Mary. The old bitch wouldn't act this way if I were Ruth."

"Well, that's one thing you don't have to worry about," Tully said. "You're not."

His tone seemed to calm her down. "I know I'm not, Davey. It's been thrown up to me all my life. What the hell happened to this drink?" She went over to the bar and got busy again. "It's always been Ruth this and Ruth that, all that's pure and holy. In Mercedes's case it's easy to understand — she latched onto Ruth as a substitute for her daughter Kathleen, who becomes more and more of a saint the longer she's dead — in Mercedes's mind, that is." Sandra Jean took her fresh drink to the sofa and curled up opposite him. "That's all right with me. . . ."

"I don't think it is," Tully said. "I think you hate Ruth. I think you've always hated her."

Sandra Jean looked into her tall glass and considered this. "Maybe I do at that," she said at last. "Maybe I always have, as you say. And that makes me out a stinker for real, doesn't it?"

"Forget it," Tully said, barely waving his hand. "Forget it. I hardly know what I'm saying."

"Look, Davey," the girl said, setting her glass down on the floor. He looked, and he saw a Sandra Jean ten years older, her face drawn down in bitter lines. "Did Ruth ever tell you that our mother died giving birth to me? Till the day he died Daddy never forgave me for it — I was the 'cause,' you see, for Mother's dying. Poor Daddy had a tough time trying not to show it, and it'll give you a short idea of the kind of cookie our father was when I tell you that his solution was to pretend I wasn't there. So I never had a mother, and to my father I was a sort of nothing. Naturally, he gave all his paternal attention — and love — to Ruth, who could do no wrong. That's what I grew up with — a guilt feeling about my mother's death and having my big sister thrown in my face. And it's still going on."

"I didn't know that." Tully shaded his burning eyes. He had never more than tolerated Sandra Jean, being polite to her only for his wife's sake; but now he realized that for some time he had even stopped thinking of the girl as a human being. She had become a sort of ambulatory annoyance — a tart-tongued irritant when her sister was around, a menace when she could corner him alone. He could not even flatter himself that she was sexually attracted to him. It was Sandra Jean's way of tearing down everything around her that seemed to have some solidity. Now he understood why. "I'm sorry we haven't got on better, Sandra," Tully said.

"Are you now," the girl said. She had been biting her lips; but now she retracted them in a curl of malice. She stooped and snatched up her glass. "And I love you, too, Davey my lad. *Pros't!*" She tossed down the contents of the glass and deliberately dropped it on the sofa and jumped up. "On that moon-eyed note, dear brother-in-law, you are rid of me for the evening. Any more of it and I'll throw up."

"Where are you going?" It was her way of covering up, he knew, for having momentarily exposed herself.

"Back to the Cabbotts' to play hell with Mercedes's plans. She has no intention of turning Andy loose on an unsuspecting world, but the dumb bunny may not realize it unless there's someone there to tell him. And that's me. Say, call me a cab, will you? I was expecting Andy to drive me back."

Tully silently rose and went into his den and phoned for a taxi. When he returned she was standing at the front door. "You're not such a bad egg, Davey," she said brightly. "Only a little on the raunchy side . . . I had you going with all that autobiographical crud, didn't I, Dave boy?"

"It sounded real to me," Tully smiled faintly.

His smile infuriated her.

"So what!" Sandra Jean snarled. "I don't need you, Ruth or anybody else!"

About ten minutes after Sandra Jean drove away in the cab, the phone rang in the study. Tully raced for it.

"Yes?" he said hoarsely.

"Dave? Julian Smith."

Tully sagged. The detective's tone was good for nothing but more bad news.

"Did Ruth — did you — ?"

"No, Dave," Smith said. "No sign of her yet . . . Dave."

"Yes, Julian."

"I'm afraid I've sat on this just as long as it could be sat on. The *Times-Call* and the TV people have it. I simply couldn't keep Ruth's name out of it any longer."

"Thanks anyway, Julian. You've been more than considerate."

"They'll be on your neck any minute. . . . I don't suppose *you've* heard from Ruth?" the Homicide man said suddenly.

"No."

"Dave —"

"I said no!" Tully cried. "God damn it, don't you understand English?"

Smith hung up softly and, after a moment, Tully followed suit. His hands were shaking violently. He was heading for the

Scotch when the doorbell chimed.

Tully changed course and sneaked a look out the picture window.

Any minute was right. They were here. The press *and* the TV together. He opened the door.

One of them was the city editor of the *Times-Call*, in person; the other was chief of the news staff of the local television station. David Tully knew them both well. Jake Ballinger was a rumpled, baggy-pantsed old newspaperman from Chicago who had chosen to finish off his illustrious career on a small-town paper; Eddie Harper was a prematurely bald young TV flash who had put the local station on the state map in a big way. If Ballinger and Harper were covering the Cox story in person, Ruth and he were in for it.

They treated Tully very gently, offering sincere-sounding regrets for the occasion of their visit, easing into their questions:

— What do you know about this?

Nothing. I got back from upstate and walked right into the middle of it. I don't know any more about it than you do.

— Where is Mrs. Tully?

I don't know.

— You must have heard from her.

No.

— She didn't leave you a note or anything?

*No. But my wife is innocent. That's the only
thing I'm sure of.*

— What makes you so sure?

Ruth couldn't murder anybody.

— Then you have no proof that Mrs.
Tully didn't shoot this man Cox?

*I don't need proof. I know her better than
anyone in the world. This is all a terrible
mixup — mistake of some kind. It will be
cleared up when she's found.*

— But you have no idea where she is?

No. I told you.

— And you haven't any clue to her
present whereabouts?

No, I said!

— How long has Mrs. Tully known
Crandall Cox? (this was Jake Ballinger, so-
licitously.)

*I'm not answering any Did-you-stop-
beating-your-wife type questions! She didn't
know him! At all!*

— Do you know that for a fact?

*No, I don't know it for a fact — how could
I? I know it because she never mentioned a
name remotely like that!*

— But she must have known him, Mr.
Tully (this was the TV news chief, gently).
Cox called her by name, according to the

witness the police have. By her first name, as I understand it.

— And your gun was used, Dave.

— So Mrs. Tully must have been there, wouldn't you say, Mr. Tully?

I'm saying nothing further — nothing at all!

When the two newsmen were gone, Tully poured himself a stiff shot, and another, and then another. He had handled himself badly, he knew. Done Ruth's cause an actual disservice. Most of all, perhaps, he had resented their pity, as Sandra Jean had resented his.

Standing at the window with the third drink in his hand, Tully felt emotionally naked. Where *was* Ruth? What was she doing? And why? Ruth's cause . . . Did she have a cause?

He tried to keep his thoughts at bay, but they kept hurtling through his mind: Is she only a smoother version of Sandra Jean . . . conning me . . . insinuating herself into Mercedes Cabbott's affections by playing on the old woman's memory of a dead daughter . . . fooling the whole town . . . until an unsavory chapter in her past caught up with her . . . ?

The phone rang again. He rushed into the den.

"Hello!"

"The Tully residence?" It was a woman's voice, the wrong woman's. "This is Miss Blake."

"Who? Oh, from the Hobby Motel. Yes?"

"I ain't there any more, Mr. Tully. I just moved to Flynn's Inn — too many rubbernecks at the motel. Look, I read the paper. First time I saw you I figured you for class, and now I see by the paper that I was right — you're a real big shot around here."

"What do you want?" Tully asked curtly.

"Well, now, you know I told you I'd think real hard about Cranny Cox. I like to help people if I can."

"Sure you do, Miss Blake." He braced himself; this might be genuine, at that. "And you do remember something now?"

"Why don't you come over to Flynn's Inn and we'll talk about it?"

"Do you know where my wife is?"

"I didn't say *that.*"

"Do you!"

She sounded quite unperturbed by his violence. "I like to see who I'm talking to. You better come over here."

"What's your room number?"

She laughed. "Room two two two. Just you come on up . . . alone, Mr. Tully."

"What are you afraid of, Miss Blake?"

For a wild instant he suspected some sort of trap.

"Witnesses," she said simply. "You say nothing to nobody and come alone, mister, or don't bother to come at all."

8

She was waiting for him in the doorway of her room. He supposed she had instructed the seedy clerk at the desk in the dusty lobby to warn her of his arrival.

Stretched over her gelatinous figure were skintight slimjims with a pattern of huge pink roses and a knit blouse that sculptured her outsized chest. There was a cigarette in her fat fingers and a tobacco crumb on her lips.

"Anybody with you?" She stepped into the hall and glanced down the dingy stairwell.

"You said to come alone."

She motioned him into her room and followed him in.

She shut and latched the door and leaned back against it, watching him critically — even, Tully thought, anxiously. He glanced around the room; he had never set foot in Flynn's Inn before. Like the hall it was dingy and cramped and dirty, and she had brought with her from the motel room the same odor of stale smoke and cheap perfume. He wondered if he was the intended victim of a badger game — the bed was unmade, the bedclothes tumbled about.

"Have a drink, Mr. Tully?"

"What? Oh — no, thanks. Miss Blake —"

"I never been much on this 'Miss Blake' stuff." The woman went to the dusty bureau and poured herself a shot from a two-thirds empty fifth of rye. "You call me Maudie."

"Look," Tully said. "I don't know what you're up to, but if this is some kind of shakedown racket —"

"Why, Mr. Tully, you got no right to talk to me like that!" She actually sounded injured. "I just had a story to tell you."

"Then tell it, please, and I'll get out of here."

"A real sad story, I mean." She slung the contents of the shot glass down her throat. "About a girl who needs a loan."

"I'm not a banker or a money-lender," Tully said shortly. "I'm in the market for information and I'll buy it. How much do you want?" He brought out his wallet and waited. Her quick animal eyes pounced on it and sprang away. She went back to the bureau and refilled the glass.

"What's your hurry, Mr. Tully? Why don't you sit down and relax?" Tully looked around, spotted one uncluttered chair, and sat down on it. "That's better," she smiled. "You see, Mr. Tully, I leveled with the cops. My neck ain't stuck out. If I happen to remember an extra detail later, that's natural, ain't it?"

"What detail?"

Her glance was fixed on his right hand, and he looked down. He had forgotten that he was still holding the wallet. "First about that loan I mentioned . . ."

He made an impatient gesture. "How much?"

Maudie Blake said swiftly, "A hundred. Cash. They don't like checks here."

Tully opened his wallet and leafed through its contents. There were three twenties and a few small bills. "All I have on me is seventy-eight dollars."

She walked over to him and deliberately looked into his wallet. "Okay," she said. "Gimme."

He handed her the bills and put his empty wallet away. She made a tight roll of the money and thrust it into the cleft under her blouse.

"Well?" Tully demanded. He felt himself sweating.

She carried her drink to a lumpy chair and sat down, draping her left leg over the arm. She looked at him uneasily and gulped the whisky. She had apparently been drinking for some time; her eyes were beginning to blear and she sounded a little tight.

"You're not going to like this, Mr. Tully," the woman began slowly. "Remember, I never promised you would. Right?"

"If it's about Crandall Cox," Tully said, "I'm listening."

"And your wife." She blinked and tongued her lips. "She wasn't the only one," she said. "A long time ago . . . well, Cranny used to tell me he didn't give a damn about any of them but me. I didn't believe him even then. But — you know how dames are, Mr. Tully. Or maybe you don't."

Or maybe I don't . . .

Maudie Blake's face drooped all over. "I was the one who was always there — he always had me, and he knew it. Cranny Cox was the kind needed a woman to fall back on when he was scared or broke — something like a dog he could count on no matter what he did. A dog that didn't ask for nothing but a pat on the head once in a while, or even a boot in the rear."

She got up and shuffled back to the bureau and the whisky bottle.

"It must have been rough on you," Tully

said. Who cares? he thought. Get on with it!

"Rough? Yes, you could say that, mister . . . yess'r, you could sure say that."

He thought she was going to cry. Instead, her mouth tightened and she seized the bottle and drank directly from it and then took it back to the lumpy chair with her.

"When he got real sick this last time," she said, "I figured I had Cranny for good. Though what I wanted with him I can't tell you. All I knew was . . . I'd sooner have a kick from Cranny Cox than a kiss from any other man I ever knew. And *he* knew it. Goddam that ugly creep, he knew it!"

"Miss Blake," Tully said. "Maudie —"

But she mumbled, "And I was wrong again. I didn't have him, any more than the other times. He still had his great big plans to live it up. He just let me take care of him till he could get back on his feet. Then he robbed me and took off again."

In spite of the sick dread in the pit of his stomach Tully found himself becoming aware of Maudie Blake as a woman, a hopeless addict of what she herself would hardly dare call love — love for a man who permitted her to shelter and nurse and feed him and give him money, and who then deserted her again.

"Did you know his plans? That he was coming here?"

"He didn't tell me nothing. One day I come home and he was gone, and he didn't come back. No note, no nothing. But I found a bus timetable . . . he'd marked it . . . name of a town, and I remembered he'd once said it was his home town."

"So you followed him?"

"Took the next bus." She hiccupped and giggled, " *'Scuse* me."

"Why?"

"Huh?" She peered at him owlishly.

"Why did you follow him?"

She seemed surprised. "He needed me."

"If he left you without a word," Tully said, "how did you know he was at the Hobby?" Suddenly he was suspicious.

"I didn't. But I figured him for a cheap motel — I'd only left a few bucks in my flat that he'd lifted. Third motel I tried, there he was, walking across the parking lot."

"I suppose he wasn't very glad to see you?"

"He cussed me out good." She laughed, tilted the bottle again. But it was empty, and she flung it from her. "Later he says okay, you're here you can stay, only keep out of my hair." She laughed again, then scowled and began to struggle out of the chair. "I got to get me another bottle —"

But Tully was towering over her, and she plopped back in alarm. "Cox told you why he'd come here, didn't he?"

"No —"

"You're lying. You've known all along, haven't you?"

Through her fright he saw a glint of cunning. "That ain't what you're buying for seventy-eight bucks, Mr. Tully."

"Would you rather Lieutenant Smith asked you the question?"

"You yell copper and a fat lot of good it'll do you," she muttered. "I'd just have to tell him like I'm telling you: I don't know why Cranny came here, I just followed him, that's all. Is there a law against that?"

Something in Tully's face above her sobered her.

"Now don't you try muscle on me, mister!"

"Cox told you his plan, didn't he?"

"He never —"

"And I was beginning to feel sorry for you! Either you were both in on this from the start, or he cut you in on the action when you showed up at the Hobby!"

She shrank deep into the chair. "No. I swear —"

"Making you share the crime of whatever he was up to would be a kind of insurance for Cox. That's it, isn't it? He didn't trust you, so he assigned part of the job to you. What were you supposed to do, Maudie?" Tully was shaking her now, his fingers deep in her fat shoulders. "What part of the mucky plan did he assign to you? Talk, you bitch!"

It was the sight of her eyes that brought him to his senses. They were bugging out, terrified, from her purpling face; and to Tully's horror he saw that his hands were around her neck. He released her and backed off. She felt her throat unbelievingly.

"You were gonna choke me," she whispered. "I ought to have you arrested for f'lonious assault, that's what I ought to do! . . . But I got a better idea, Mr. Tully."

She was all bitch now, a mountain of triumphant flesh. Tully half turned away, half closed his smarting eyes. The Blake woman got out of the chair and waddled over to him, still feeling her neck.

"I was trying to ease you into it because I thought you were real class and a nice guy and I didn't want to hurt you no more than I had to. But now, Mr. Tully, I'm gonna give it to you good! You know what your seventy-eight bucks bought? You listen!"

He tried to avoid her sour breath, but he could not.

"You drive on up to the Lodge at Wilton Lake — the Lodge, hear? Talk to the people who run it — the maids and the bellhops — take a good long look at the register —"

"What are you talking about?" Tully stammered. "The register for when — what?"

"Two summers ago — first week in June, Mr. Tully," the woman jeered. "Him and her — yeah! Cranny Cox and your wife."

Tully became aware of his surroundings. He was seated behind the wheel of his car in the parking lot of Flynn's Inn. A man came staggering out of the bar and a blare of drunken noise came out with him. Then the door closed and everything was silent again.

He had no recollection of leaving Maudie Blake's room or of getting into the Imperial. He remembered only the ghost of a cackle behind him, as if some witch had laughed in a nightmare . . .

He lit a cigarette mechanically.

The Blake woman was a vicious liar, of course. It couldn't possibly be true. To shack up at a resort hotel with a rotten

110

punk like Crandall Cox. . . . Impossible. Not Ruth. Not a woman as fastidious as Ruth.

Then why had she gone running to the Hobby Motel at Cox's call . . . with a gun . . . two years later?

There's a reason, Tully thought desperately. There's got to be a reason — a reason that takes me off this hook — a reason a man could live with . . .

One thing is sure, he told himself. I know my wife. I'm not going to give that sodden bag of lard the satisfaction of having made me drive up to Wilton Lake on a sneak check. . . .

Two summers ago . . . that was before their marriage, before they had even met. Maybe Ruth *had* been there at the Lodge at the same time as Cox, so what? It could have been the frankest coincidence, something the jealous mind of this Blake virago had seized and built on to house her jealousy. Or else Cox, having met Ruth casually, had done the building to torment Maudie Blake, in the sadistic way of kept men contemptuously sure of their keepers. That was it! Cox had made up the whole story and spilled it to Maudie Blake for laughs, knowing she would fall for it and agonize over it.

So it wouldn't really be doubting Ruth if he did drive up to the Lake and sort of got the feel of the place again. Tully began to think about it even pleasurably. He hadn't been up to the Lake in years . . .

And, of course! He sat up in the car, tingling.

If Ruth *had* spent some time at Wilton Lake two summers ago she could hardly have failed, in her instinctive appreciation of nature, to fall under its spell. It was a beautiful, serene, secluded place, not over-patronized, and at this particular season . . . Why, she might be up there right now! Frightened, maybe, not knowing what to do, not daring to phone, hoping against hope that somehow he would fathom her hide-out and come secretly to her rescue . . .

What am I waiting for? Tully asked himself exultantly.

As he started his car he shut down his mind, refusing to think past the point at which he had stopped.

9

The distance from town to the Lake was a hundred and sixty miles. Tully covered it in under three hours, taking the final twists of the mountain road shortly after nine o'clock.

The Lodge lay at the northern end of the great lake — a rugged, spreading two-story ranch building of ivy-overgrown fieldstone and hand-hewn logs. The west terrace was lighted with copper torches. Cooks in tall chef's hats were serving an outdoor barbecue to the music of a strolling trio of cowboy-clad guitarists. Half the terrace tables were unoccupied.

The beamed lobby with its great fieldstone fireplaces was quiet. An attractive woman of middle age was on duty behind the desk.

"I was to meet my wife here," Tully said. "Do you have a Mrs. Tully registered?"

The woman consulted a register-file. "I'm sorry, sir, she hasn't arrived yet. If you have a reservation, would you like to register for the two of you?"

"No. I want to see the manager."

Tully was hungry-faced and gray. The woman hesitated.

"It's important."

She looked him over carefully. "Just a moment, please." She lifted the wicket, crossed the lobby and disappeared through the tall doors that led to the terrace.

She came back several minutes later with a sunburned young man. He smiled and said, "I'm the manager of the Lodge, Mr. Tully — Dalrymple is the name. Don't worry about your wife's not getting here on schedule. It happens all the time."

"May I speak to you in private, Mr. Dalrymple?"

The young manager's smile became rather fixed.

"Of course. This way, please."

In his office, Dalrymple offered Tully a chair. Tully shook his head, and the manager chose to remain standing, too. He was no longer smiling at all. "I really don't see what the problem is, sir, if it's merely a matter of your wife's being delayed —"

"She may be here already," Tully said.

"I beg your pardon?"

"Registered under another name."

The manager now sat down, slowly. "I see," he said. "I see . . . Of course, Mr. Tully, the management can't accept the least responsibility —"

"I'm not asking you to accept any responsibility. I'm not here to make trouble," Tully said. He pulled his wallet from his pocket and showed Dalrymple a clear snapshot of Ruth. "This is my wife, Mr. Dalrymple. All I want to know: Is she here? Under any name?"

The manager accepted the wallet photo and sat studying it a moment. "No, sir."

"Are you sure?"

"Positive. We're not a large hotel. Vacationers are our stock in trade, and I make it my business to know every guest. I assure you, your wife isn't registered under her own or any other name."

The manager was smiling again. He started to rise. "If that's all, Mr. Tully . . ."

"It's not."

The manager remained in mid-rise.

Tully's pallor had taken on a haggard caste. "Two summers ago . . . the first week of June . . . May I see your register for that period?"

"Certainly not!" The manager completed his rise as if a spring had been released.

"I'll have to insist, Mr. Dalrymple."

"It's absolutely against our rules! I'm sorry, sir —"

"Would you rather I ask the police to take a look for me?"

"Police?" Dalrymple blinked. "Of course, if a crime has been committed — although I assure you, sir, no crime has ever been committed on these premises! —"

"I didn't say it was."

"What kind of crime?" the manager asked abruptly.

Tully hesitated. Then he shrugged. "Murder."

Mr. Dalrymple went oyster-white. "How is the Lodge involved?"

"There's a question as to whether or not a certain man and . . ." Tully licked his lower lip ". . . and the original of this photo visited the Lodge two years ago . . . together . . . or at least at the same time. If I can check it out here and now, Mr. Dalrymple, the police may never come into it at all. Of course, I can't guarantee that. Do you let me see your register or don't you?"

The manager stared at Tully for a long time. Tully withstood his calculating appraisal with indifference. A numbness was setting in, not so much a lack of feeling as a suspension of it.

"Well?"

Dalrymple's glance wavered to Ruth's photo, which was still on the desk between them. He sat down and began to scrutinize it very carefully. "This woman — I mean your wife, Mr. Tully — is she . . . ?"

"Yes." He almost started to add, *But that was before I married her.*

"Two summers ago, eh? I must say the face looks familiar . . . The trouble is, I see so many people come and go —" He rose again, handed the snapshot back to Tully. "What was the man's name?"

Tully found himself able to say, "Cox. Crandall Cox," without choking.

"Wait here, please."

Dalrymple left, shutting the door emphatically behind him. Tully remained where he was. He had not shifted his position six inches since entering the office. He simply stood there, not thinking.

When the manager returned he had with him a dumpy gray-haired woman wearing old-fashioned gold-rimmed eyeglasses.

"Well?" Tully said.

"Well!" Dalrymple inhaled. He said quickly, "We had a Mr. and Mrs. Crandall Cox registered during the period you mentioned."

"How long did they stay?"

"Three days." The man gestured, and the gray-haired woman stumped forward; she had badly flat feet, Tully noticed, and then he wondered what difference that made, what difference anything made.

"This is Mrs. Hoskins, one of our maids, Mr. Tully. Employed here fourteen years. Two years ago she worked the wing where Mr. and Mrs. — where this couple had their suite."

"Suite," Tully said.

"I remember them, all right," the woman said. She had a flat-footed kind of voice, too, as if she had never learned to use it right. "He was the man took an afternoon nap with a cigarette in his hand and he burned the new couch in the suite, Mr. Dalrymple, you remember. He'd tied a real good one on —"

"Yes, yes, Mrs. Hoskins, thank you," Dalrymple said.

Tully forced himself to take the photo of Ruth from the desk and across the room to Mrs. Hoskins.

"Is this the woman?"

Mrs. Hoskins adjusted her glasses and peered earnestly. "Looks like her. Yes, sir, I'd say she was the one. It's been a long time, but I always remembered that couple real well even though they was here such a short time. Something about them two —"

"What?" Tully said.

"Well, for one thing, most of the guests the Lodge gets don't drink so much. More refined, like."

Dalrymple coughed nervously. Tully took the photo of Ruth from the woman's worked-out fingers and replaced it in his wallet. He was surprised to find that his own hands were perfectly steady. "Do you remember anything else about them?"

Mrs. Hoskins became quite animated. "Oh, yes, sir! They were real lovey-dovey. Them two are honeymooners, I says to Mrs. Biggle — she was working that wing with me then. Mrs. Biggle says, 'Whoever heard of honeymooners spending all their time getting tanked up?' but I says to her, 'It takes all kinds, and anyway I heard 'em smooching in there between drinks, like —' not," Mrs. Hoskins added hastily, "that I was listening or anything, but sometimes a maid can't help —"

"All *right*, Mrs. Hoskins," the manager said.

"I don't suppose," Tully said to the gray-haired woman, "you remember hearing the man use the woman's first name?"

"I do indeed," she said, beaming, "Ruth, it sounded like. The gentleman would say it over and over, like he liked it, too."

"That's all, that's all, Mrs. Hoskins," Dalrymple said. "Thank you."

Tully drove away from the hotel sanely

enough. But as the lights of the Lodge fell behind, his car seemed to take the bit in its teeth.

He sat like a spectator watching the mountain turns come up and past and away as if on film. Guard railings flashed by, one long blur. The Imperial's engine seemed to gather its powers and streak forward . . .

A stabbing fear jolted Tully's heart.

He jerked his foot from the accelerator in sheer reflex. And went limp and cold.

He drove the rest of the way at a crawl.

The house loomed remote, strange . . . still dark. He got out of the car heavily and let himself in.

As he trudged about turning on lights, the thought came to him that he had forgotten to eat anything. Without hunger he went into the kitchen, put together a sandwich, and sat munching.

The testimony of Maudie Blake might be suspect. But not that of the Lodge manager and the gray-haired maid.

And yet, Tully told himself, it doesn't fit, it simply doesn't fit. Ruth, even a single Ruth, spending three days at a resort hideaway with a man like Cox! Unless she was a sort of female Jekyll-Hyde. . . .

The phone rang. Tully put aside the half-eaten sandwich and got up from the kitchen table and went to the wall extension.

"Yes?" He no longer had any real hope that the answering voice might be Ruth's.

"Dave? Norma." Norma Hurst's voice was calmer than usual. Thank you, Lord, thought Tully, for small miracles. "I've been trying to get you."

"I was out, Norma. Anything special?"

"No," Ollie Hurst's wife said, "it's just that I haven't had a chance to talk to you since the news about — since the news. I don't suppose you've heard anything?"

"No."

Norma was silent. Then she said, "Dave, I want you to know we're all with you. I just don't believe Ruth could be involved in a thing like this. Or, if she is, it's entirely different from the way it looks right now."

"Thanks, Norma."

He meant it. Unstable or not, Norma was a good egg. She might keep teetering on the brink of hysteria because of the brutal loss of her only child, but there was solid rock behind the thin edge.

"Norma . . . might I come over?"

"Oh, Dave, would you?"

"I mean now. I know it's late — way past midnight —"

"I insist on it! I know what it means to

be alone in the house where . . ." Norma stopped on a barely rising note. "Anyway, Ollie says he wants to talk to you — he didn't get home till an hour ago himself. Have you had anything to eat?"

"Yes, of course —"

"What?"

In spite of himself, Tully grinned. "You've got me, sister. Half a sandwich of I-don't-know-what."

"You come right over, David Tully!"

He found a four-course buffet dinner waiting for him at the Hurst house, in spite of the hour.

Norma was tall and thin and long in the face, and her brown hair was dingy with neglect. Her charm had always lain in eyes of deep beauty and the quick warmth of her smile. The smile had died with the death of her little girl; the beautiful eyes had come more and more to resemble the eyes in photos Tully had seen of Nazi concentration-camp victims — socket-sunken, enormous, haunted and haunting. But tonight she seemed a part of the existing world; Ruth's disappearance and predicament had apparently shocked her back to something like her old plain, friendly self.

Ollie made a great show of being normal, but his always restless hands were busier than ever tonight, feeling, pulling, scratching, rubbing — and the light bounced off his freckled skull like a yellow warning signal.

But there was reassurance in seeing Norma and Ollie together. Angular Norma, plain and warm as home-made bread; stocky Ollie, shrewd, transparent-eyed, in perpetual motion — it had always been hard for Tully to imagine them not married to each other. They were complementary; they had a mutual need, yet an individual stamp. Ollie Hurst had been a hole-in-the-shoe student; Norma had a comfortable income from stocks and real estate she had inherited. Norma herself had once told Tully that Ollie had never touched a penny of her money; it had been a condition of their marriage, at his unarguable insistence.

Ruth and I had some pleasant times in this house, Tully thought. Before little Emmie died. Before Ruth . . .

He shut down tight on that one.

It was impossible to recreate the past, in spite of Norma's surprising recapture of her old self. She fed Tully quietly, while her husband tried to make small talk. But the food stuck in Tully's throat, and Ollie seemed to dry up, and finally an awkward silence fell.

"Suppose we face this instead of pretending it hasn't happened and that Ruth's here," Norma said.

Ollie said, "Nor . . ."

"Oh, shut up, Ollie, this is no time for your office psychology. You do it badly, anyway, when your emotions are involved . . . David." Norma Hurst touched Tully's hand. "Don't lose faith in her."

Tully was grateful. "What do we do about the evidence, Norma? Ignore it?"

"Yes," Norma said, "until Ruth has a chance to explain."

"Cox is no foggy abstract who'll dry up with the sunrise. Cox is real. Or was."

"So is Ruth, Dave. And she still is."

"Norma," Ollie said. "Maybe Dave doesn't want to talk about it."

"I think he does. I think it will do him good. Don't you want to talk, Dave?"

"I need to do more than talk," Tully muttered.

"You need to know you're not alone," Norma said. Her eyes retreated for a moment. "I know."

But now it all came back in a rush, and Tully cried, "She knew Cox. That's a fact. A *fact*."

"How do you know that, Dave?" the lawyer asked quickly.

"Never mind —"

"I don't care what you say," Norma said, and there was a strange tautness in her voice that pulled even Tully around. "Even if she did know him, she's innocent. I won't believe anything else!"

The two men exchanged glances. Then Tully got up and went over to Norma and stooped and kissed her on the forehead. "Of course, Norma, of course. You're a good friend. A great comfort."

But she sat like stone. The old look of panic appeared in her husband's eyes.

"I'm really pooped," Tully said. "I'd better pop back home and hit the sack. Thanks, Norm, for the feed. Ollie —"

"I'll see you out," Ollie said. "Be right back, Nor." At the door he said in a low voice, "Now don't blame yourself, Dave. This has been coming on all day."

"Norma said you wanted to talk to me —"

"I'll drop by in the morning." The lawyer shut the door swiftly. Through the big window as he passed Tully saw Ollie taking his wife's hand with great gentleness. Norma was sitting as they had left her, without expression, except that tears were inching down her face.

10

David Tully had just finished his lonely breakfast when Ollie Hurst drove up. He came in wiping his cranium with a folded handkerchief. His eyes were bloodshot from lack of sleep.

"How's Norma, Ollie?"

"She had a bad night. Apparently this business of Ruth is somehow tied up in her mind with Emmie's death. I finally got her under sedation and asleep, and she seems a lot better this morning."

"I'm sorry as hell, Ollie —"

"Forget it," the lawyer said abruptly. "If it hadn't been that it would have been something else. How about some of that coffee I smell?"

"I've been keeping it hot for you."

They went into the kitchen and Tully poured coffee into two fresh cups.

"No," Ollie said, refusing the cream and sugar, which he usually used in immoderate proportions, "I need it straight this morning," and he gulped a third of it and set his cup down and said, "Anything on Ruth yet?"

"No."

"Dave."

"Yes?"

"Do you know where she is? Are you hiding her?"

Tully glared into the lawyer's crystal eyes. "No. *No.*"

"Okay, okay," Hurst said. "I had to be sure. And you still haven't heard from her?"

"No."

"All right. Then let's talk about the future."

"The future of what?" Tully asked bitterly.

"The future of Ruth."

"What future?"

"Oh, the hell with that defeatist talk," Ollie Hurst snapped. "Look, Dave, I'm a lawyer, and I'm your and Ruth's friend. If you want to wallow in hopelessness that's your funeral — and incidentally it only makes my job tougher. Now what's it going to be? Do I have to do this with you on my back, dead weight, or are we in this together?"

Tully stiffened.

"That's right, hate my guts," Ollie said. "I don't mind. All right. Now I've got us a good criminal lawyer, I mean on tap. I've retained him tentatively, and I've talked the whole thing over with him as it stands. He agrees that there's no point in his coming into this until Ruth turns up or is found. Do you want to know who he is?"

Tully shook his head.

"You mean you actually trust somebody besides yourself? I swan to Marthy! Anyway, his name is Vinzenti and he's top dog upstate in trial work, especially murder cases. I've got to be frank with you, Dave. Vinzenti says that unless Ruth can come up with clear counter-evidence to refute the facts as they now seem to stand, we'll have a real fight on our hands. He also said that the longer she remains in hiding the worse it's going to look for her. That's why I had to ask you again if you know where she is."

"I told you I *don't.*"

"I believe you, Dave," the lawyer said soothingly. "I'm just outlining the situation. How about a refill?"

Tully replenished Hurst's cup.

"You haven't touched yours."

Tully drank it.

"The circumstantial case against Ruth is strong," Ollie Hurst went on. "The use of your gun, the testimony of a witness who overheard Cox call his woman-visitor Ruth — and especially Ruth's disappearance after the shooting, add up to a pretty powerful prosecutor's case, according to Vinzenti.

"Against this, he says — barring some unforeseeable explanation when Ruth turns up that automatically clears her — the defense will have to try to tear down the evidence. The typewritten unsigned letter, Vinzenti thinks, for instance, is inadmissible, unless the police have turned up an identifiable fingerprint of Ruth's on it. Most of all Vinzenti seems to be counting on the human element. This may well turn out to be, he says, one of those cases in which the law and the evidence prove of less weight than the character of the people involved. The professional leech who preyed on women, the woman of refinement and good reputation who in panic and desperation turned on the beast who was trying to wreck her life — in a setup like that, juries always empathize with the woman, Vinzenti assured me."

Tully laughed. The lawyer looked at him sharply.

"What was that for, Dave?"

"Nothing." A woman of refinement and good reputation, Tully thought. Wait till the prosecution gets hold of that Lodge shack-up!

"The hell you say. Dave, if there's something you're holding back . . ."

Tully shook his head. He could not, he could not talk about Ruth and Cox and those three days at the Lodge two years before. Not now. Not yet.

Ollie Hurst continued to study him. Finally, he shrugged. "If you are, Dave, you're being a very foolish guy. Well, we'll have to trust your judgment. Isn't there anything new you can tell me?"

"Yes," Tully said. "We may find help in an unexpected place."

"What do you mean?"

"I've had a session with that witness — the woman, Maudie Blake. She told me something she didn't tell Julian Smith."

"Oh?"

"She and Crandall Cox were old buddy-buddies. He shacked up with her whenever he was on his uppers, or in trouble. The last time he was sick, he let her take care of him till he could get back on his feet, then he lifted some money she'd left around and took off for here. And she followed him. That's how she came to be in the next room at the Hobby."

"She told you all this?"

"That's right."

"Well," the lawyer said softly. "That's

interesting. How come she told you, Dave, and not the police?"

"They didn't pay her. I did."

"She asked you for money?"

"Yes."

"How much?"

"A hundred dollars. I only had seventy-eight with me. She took it."

The bald lawyer frowned. He got up and began to walk around the kitchen, pulling his nose, scratching his ear, frowning.

"I don't know, Dave," he said slowly. "That's pretty valuable information to sell for seventy-eight dollars. Unless she's stupid and cheap as hell —"

"She is." Tully wondered what he would say if he knew what else Maudie Blake had sold for the same seventy-eight dollars.

"Did you tell this to Lieutenant Smith?"

"No. Anyway, she said if I told the police she'd simply deny the whole story and stand pat on her original testimony."

Hurst kept shaking his head. "I still don't like it. If she's telling the truth she can deny her head off — the facts can be dug up. She can't be *that* stupid. Dave, you're not telling me the whole story."

"All right, I'm not," Tully burst out. "But don't ask me to talk about the rest — not yet, Ollie. The point is, she can be

131

bought. In fact, I was intending to see her again this morning after you left. I think she knows a hell of a lot more than she told even me."

"You may be getting into something you can't handle, Dave," the lawyer said. "I'd better go with you."

Tully hesitated.

"Maybe I ought to put it this way, Dave," his friend said gently. "If I'm going to help you, I can't do it in the dark, and I'm certainly not going to get a man with Vinzenti's reputation into a case where the defendant's husband is withholding information. Am I in, or out?"

Tully was quiet.

Then his shoulders drooped and he said, "All right, Ollie."

They went in Ollie Hurst's car. Ollie drove, and neither man uttered a sound all the way.

The lawyer parked in the lot beside Flynn's Inn and they got out and went into the dust-dancing lobby.

The same seedy clerk was behind the desk, picking his teeth with a green plastic toothpick while he read a comic book called *She-Cat of Venus*.

"Miss Blake," Tully said. "Maudie Blake?"

"So?" the clerk said.

"She in?"

"Mm-hm," the clerk said, turning a page. "At least I ain't seen her come down. She's one of those afternoon getter-uppers, I guess."

They walked up to the second floor. Tully led the way to the woman's door and rapped. He rapped again.

"She must be sleeping off a drunk," he said to Hurst. "She was tying one on last night when I saw her." He rapped again, shook his head, tried the door. It was locked, and he rattled the knob. "Miss Blake? Maudie?"

"When she ties one on it stays tied, doesn't it?"

"Maybe we'd better come back later, Ollie."

"Let's not and say we did," the lawyer said grimly. He banged on the door with his fist. "Miss Blake!"

There was no response.

"How about asking the desk clerk to ring her room?" Tully suggested.

Ollie Hurst hurried downstairs. A moment later Tully heard the muffled ringing. It kept ringing. Finally it stopped.

Tully began to nurse an uneasy feeling. Ollie was coming back up the stairs with the clerk. They were arguing.

"But I ain't supposed to do that, Mr. Hurst," the clerk was protesting. Apparently Ollie had told the Venusian enthusiast who he was.

"She may be seriously ill," Ollie said. "Suppose she's in a coma or something?"

"Coma my eye," the clerk grumbled; he had a key with him. "This broad's been lappin' it up like a camel since she got here. If I get into trouble over this, boy —"

"You won't," Tully said. "Open it up."

The clerk unlocked the door, pushed it open a bit, and poked his head into the room.

"Miss Blake — ?"

His head retracted like a turtle's. He made a gagging sound and rushed down the stairs.

Tully kicked the door wide.

She was lying in an impossible position on the bed, twisted like a contortionist from the waist down, head hanging far over the side. She was wearing the skintight slimjims with the enormous pink rose design and the knit blouse, just as she had been dressed when he had seen her the day before. The only change was that her feet were bare; one shoe lay near the bed, the other was half under the radiator near

134

the window. Apparently in an alcoholic collapse she had fallen across the bed, kicking her shoes off as she did so.

A three-quarters-empty bottle of whisky was lying on its side near her right hand. Only a little of it had soaked into the bed.

Neither man made a move to enter the room; they could see only too well from the doorway.

Her synthetic gold hair hung straight down, almost touching the floor; at the roots it was a dirty brown. There was a fish-belly gray-blueness about her stiffened face, a brownish crust at one corner of her open mouth. Her eyes were open, too, staring at infinity.

"That," Tully said with a laugh, "is what you might call dead to the world. How lucky can I get?"

"Dave." Ollie Hurst grasped his arm.

"Don't worry. I have no intention of going in there."

"Dave," the lawyer said again. Tully stepped back and stood slackly in the hall. Hurst reached in, grasped the knob, and pulled the door to. "We'd better notify the police."

11

It was 2:00 P.M. before Julian Smith got back to his office.

Tully was seated near the lieutenant's desk. The tailored Homicide man stopped and looked at him. "Why are you still here, Dave?"

"Where else do I have to go?" Tully was slumped on his tail, his long legs stretched way out, his big hands clenched over his belt.

"How about your office?" Smith went briskly to his desk. "Your business must be going to the dogs."

"Julian, I want to talk to you."

"Sure, Dave," the detective said, glancing through a pile of reports and memoranda. "But right now I'm pretty busy —"

Tully sat up straight. Smith glanced over at him. He immediately pushed the pile of paper aside.

"Okay, Dave."

"Is there an autopsy report yet on the Blake woman?"

"Just a preliminary one."

"What's it look like?"

"The M.E. is pretty sure she died as a result of acute alcoholism. He's making the usual tests for poison, but there are no marks of violence on her, no toxic indications so far except the alcohol."

"So she's going to he written off," Tully said with a peculiar smile, "as an accidental death?"

"In all probability." Smith leaned back in his swivel chair, clasped his manicured hands behind his head. "From the empties in the room and blood analysis, she died when her intake of alcohol passed the critical point. She took one big slug too many — if she had passed out before that, she'd likely have survived. Maudie's tough luck was that she collapsed on the bed before she drank that last one. She landed on her back and she was too near unconsciousness to get up; about all she had the strength to do was lift the bottle to her mouth that last time. Her body tried to heave the stuff but, with her head way back the way it was, only an insignificant amount came up. So . . ." Julian Smith shrugged and sat up. "We get two-three deaths like that a year, Dave, even in a town of this size. Okay?"

"No," David Tully said.

"What d'ye mean no?" the detective demanded.

"I mean no, you've got it all wrong, Julian. Maudie Blake's death was not an accident. It's too damn convenient for somebody."

"Murdered, hm?" Smith seemed unexcited.

"Yes, I think she was murdered."

"And who's the somebody you think murdered her?"

"The same one who murdered Cox."

"You mean," Julian Smith said, "Ruth?"

Tully's face convulsed. He leaped to his feet, upsetting the chair. "Damn you, Julian, I *don't* mean Ruth! Ruth's the pigeon in this thing, don't you see it?"

"Dave," Smith said. "Why don't you drop by your office? Or go home and lie down? You're as wound up as an eight-day clock. What do you say?"

"No!" Tully stood glaring down at him. Suddenly he righted the overturned chair and seated himself in it. "No, Julian, I'm going to sit here till you listen to what I have to say. Or have me thrown out."

Smith hesitated. Then he smiled. "Of course I'll listen, Dave. Shoot."

Tully sat forward immediately. "I've had some time to think since this morning, and

I've doped it out. Ruth didn't fire that shot. Someone else did. *Maudie Blake knew that* — knew who really murdered Cox. She implicated Ruth to cover up the killer. And when I came nosing around, Maudie tightened the noose around Ruth's neck to keep me off the right track."

"You mean by sending you up to Wilton Lodge, Dave?"

Tully blinked. "You knew that?"

"I've had one of my men tailing you. We know you went to see Maudie Blake yesterday. We know you then drove up to the Lodge. After you left there, my man tackled the manager. Dalrymple was quite cooperative."

"It's too damn bad," Tully said thickly, "your man didn't stick around Flynn's Inn instead. The Blake woman would still be alive!"

Lieutenant Smith frowned the least bit. "I don't see that that kind of talk is going to get us anywhere, Dave. What's your point?"

"Don't you see it? Why Maudie sent me up to the Lodge? She wasn't interested in the lousy hundred bucks she asked me for, or the seventy-eight I was actually able to cough up. She was after a goldmine! That Wilton Lodge business strengthens the circumstantial case against Ruth. It sends me off in the wrong direction. To that extent it protects the real killer better, and so ups the value of what Maudie's selling. Protection, Julian — that's what she had in mind! She was going to hold what she knew over the killer's head and make him pay through the nose for keeping quiet!"

Tully stopped, out of breath, looking at Julian Smith with shining eyes. The shine slowly dulled.

"I'm sorry, Dave," Smith said, shaking his head. "I don't buy it."

"Why not, for God's sake?" Tully cried. "Doesn't it make sense?"

"As a theory, Dave, sure. But it's a theory based on pure assumption, with not a scrap of evidence or a single provable fact to support it — based on two assumptions, actually: that Ruth was not the last one to see Cox, and that Maudie Blake was murdered. There's no evidence that anyone but Ruth visited Cox on the night of his murder, and the medical findings are that the Blake woman died of overdrinking." Smith shrugged. "You know, Dave, unsupported assumptions are tricky things. I could assume something you wouldn't like."

"What's that?" Tully muttered.

"The circumstantial case against your wife rested largely on Maudie Blake's testimony as to what she overheard from her room at the Hobby Motel the night Cox was shot," the detective said. "I could assume that Ruth murdered Maudie — to get rid of a damaging witness. As a matter of fact, Dave, Maudie's death is a bad break for the State . . . and a very good one for Ruth."

Tully sat still. He had not thought of that at all.

"So, you see," Smith said mildly, "as the officer in charge of this case I'd have to welcome evidence that Maudie was murdered, because it would corroborate the assumption that she was murdered by your wife. Fortunately or unfortunately, depending on where you're sitting in this merry-go-round, Maudie was not murdered, so my assumption carries just about as much weight as yours."

Tully was silent.

"Dave, Dave," Lieutenant Smith went on in the same mild tone, "face it — tough as it is, face it. Sick, broke, Cox came back to town to blackmail Ruth. To keep him from wrecking her life, she shot him. Nothing else explains the use of your gun, taken from your house. No other motive has turned up."

Julian Smith rose. "I can't blame you for trying to find an out for Ruth. I'm sure if she were my wife I'd do the same thing — shield or no shield."

He came around the desk.

"I'll tell you what, Dave."

Tully looked up.

"Suppose I take the tail off you. I didn't like having to put you under surveillance in the first place. But in this business you either learn to treat your friends like anybody else or you turn in your shield and take up a milk route. I had to make sure. That Wilton Lodge trip of yours convinces me you really don't know where your wife is."

Tully's lips twisted. "Am I supposed to say thanks, Julian?"

The lieutenant said carefully, "I don't think I get you."

He rose. "You're telling me I'm not going to be tailed any more because you still think I know where Ruth is and may try to contact her — or she me. You're not taking the tail off me, you're doubling it." The detective's barbered cheeks began to show blood. "I don't blame *you*, Julian. You're a good cop. Let me know if you get a lead on my wife."

Julian Smith grinned faintly. "And vice versa?"

"Depends," Tully said. "It all depends."
He picked up his hat and left.

Tully let the automatic part of him take charge of the Imperial's drive home; he had other work for his conscious mind.

He kept trying to visualize the shapeless shadow of the unknown — the stealthy black blob he was now choosing to think of as the real killer of Crandall Cox and Maudie Blake.

If only he could form a picture of him . . . of it. The Blob . . .

After a while Tully gave that up as hopeless. He — it — the Blob might be anyone in the world.

He forced himself to concentrate on the crime.

The Blob had visited Cox that night at the motel after Ruth left. (To go where? But this question Tully killed dead in its tracks.) Maudie Blake overheard, recognized the voice, maybe even saw its owner as he slipped into the room, or out of it afterward. Maudie moved over to Flynn's Inn. She made contact with the killer, told him where she was, demanded a talk . . . It could have taken place either at Flynn's or elsewhere. Wherever it was, Maudie must have laid it on the line: *I know you shot Cranny Cox. I've set up this Ruth with the cops as your pigeon, and I can even make it look worse for her with what I know. But it's gonna cost . . .*

Greedy Maudie Blake. It cost, all right, but not the Blob. It cost Maudie her life. One murder or two — the penalty was the same.

It happened after I left her, Tully thought, after she sent me up to the Lodge. The Blob must have been watching, waiting. I leave, he goes in. Through a side entrance or something, unseen. Then up to her room.

She's pretty loaded by this time. He may have come prepared to strangle her, or to hit her over the head, or smother her with a pillow. But her drunken condition gives him a better idea, a way to kill her that looks like accidental death. . . .

The formless Somebody standing or sitting in Maudie's room. Maybe pretending to drink with her as he discusses her demands. Urging her to drink even more. Until she falls on the bed and passes out.

Then how easy to kill her.

The alcohol-saturated blood already poisoning her liver, kidneys, brain . . . All he has to do is to keep forcing the liquor down her throat as she lies conveniently across the bed with her head over the side

144

and her mouth open. He would have to be careful that she didn't choke to death. A little at a time . . . delicate as an operation, but easy, so easy. And finally the alcoholic content of her blood reaches and passes the fatal level.

Dead of an overdose of alcohol. What had Julian Smith said? "We get two-three deaths like that a year."

Obliterate traces of his visit. Trip the tumbler, let the door swing shut, locked.

Easy.

Safe.

(And where was Ruth all this time?)

It gnawed. It gnawed.

Shortly after Tully's return home, a sleek white sports car with the top down dragged to a stop before the house.

The screech of rubber brought him to the front window. Sandra Jean and Andrew Gordon were getting out of the car. They were talking and laughing. Mercedes Cabbott's son made a sweeping gesture: I am master of the world, it said. He stumbled slightly as they started up the walk. Tully wondered how much Andy had had to drink.

Tully opened the front door.

"Hi, pops," Sandra Jean said.

Andy made two fists, did a little shuffle, and threw a one-two at an imaginary opponent. He grinned crookedly at Tully. "Sure it's safe for me to come in, Champ? You pack a mean wallop."

"Andrew, don't be silly." Sandra Jean took him by the arm.

"Come in," Tully said.

They breezed past him into his house, Andy Gordon still shadow-boxing. He's not as drunk as he's acting, Tully thought; he rarely is.

"Oh, Andy, stop that," Sandra Jean said. "We haven't time for games. You can play all you want afterward."

"Afterward?" Tully said. He closed the front door.

"Haven't you heard?" Mercedes's son threw his head back and howled like Tarzan. "The mating call! Mind if I have two or six of your drinks?" He wobbled toward Tully's bar and got busy.

Tully glanced at Ruth's sister.

She nodded. "We're getting married, Davey."

"Oh?"

"Eloping!" the darkly handsome boy chortled. "How's that for an idea, Champ?" He threw himself into an armchair with his drink and stretched his muscular legs, grinning. Tully noticed that he merely sipped from the glass.

"Great," Tully said. "Whose idea was it?"

"Mine, o' course. Got down on my knees to my li'l ol' gal. Didn't I, sugar?" Andy rested his head on the back of the chair and began to sing *O Promise Me*. He broke off to take another sip. Tully glanced contemptuously at Sandra Jean. She laughed in his face and went over to Andy and stooped to rub cheeks with him.

"You certainly did, darling. Nicest proposal I've *ever* had. And so legal, too. Look, I'll be ready in a jiff —"

"Wait a minute," Tully said. "I take it Mercedes knows nothing about this?"

"You take it and you can have it," Andy chuckled. "I s'pose you think I'm afraid of her. No such thing, my friend. Just cutting the old umbilical. I'm old enough to know what I'm doing. Right, my-love-my-dove-my-undefiled?"

"And such muscles, too," Sandra Jean crooned.

"And what's more," the boy said, waving the glass, "if that louse of a stepfather of mine opens *his* yap — pow! I'll smear him all over the palace floor."

"You'll do no such thing," his bride-to-be smiled, laying her finger over his lips. "This is going to be a civilized elopement. No brawls, no quarrels — just sweetness and light. Mercedes doesn't mean a thing she said. All we have to do is *do* it, Andy. She won't cut you off. She'll come around."

"Not losing a son, but gaining a daughter," Andrew Gordon muttered. "I dunno though, Sandra. The old girl can get awfully tough . . ."

"Everything's going to be just fine, Andy," Sandra Jean murmured, nuzzling his ear. "You just trust Sandra Jean."

"Yeah," the boy said. He pulled her face down and kissed her fiercely.

She struggled, laughing. "Andy! In front of Dave — ?"

"Hell with Dave."

"No, now you finish your drink while I get those things together," the girl said firmly. "I'll be right back." She extricated herself, kissed him lightly on the forehead, and hurried out of the living room.

Tully followed her.

She went into his and Ruth's bedroom. Tully went in after her. She wheeled on him.

"Whatever you're intending to say, Dave — I warn you, *don't*."

"Seeing that this is my bedroom," Tully said, "do you mind if I throw up all over it?"

Her eyes, so beautiful, so like Ruth's, flashed hell's-fire. For a moment he thought she was going to spring at him claws first. But then, with remarkable discipline, she forced herself to smile.

"Davey, I'm sorry. I wouldn't have come except that I have some things of mine here I want to take with me on our honeymoon. I won't be long, and then we'll be out of your hair."

Hair. She had washed a lighter tint into her hair since he had last seen her. He wondered what its original color had been, why she kept changing it.

"Sometimes I think you're not human, Sandra."

"Mercy! And what do we mean by that?" the girl said mockingly. She looked human enough as she turned to walk across the bedroom, her hips rising and falling rhythmically. "Aren't I female-human?"

"On the outside, definitely. But what are you inside?"

"Lover, it goes clear through." She paused at the closet door — Ruth's closet — and turned around. "I know what's bugging you about me, Davey, and it hasn't a bloody thing to do with Andy Gordon or Mercedes Cabbott. You think I'm acting like a bitch because I'm proposing to run off and get married while my sister's in all this trouble. But what do you expect me to do? Sit on Mercedes's terrace and wring my hands? I told you, I can't help Ruth. All I can do is help myself. This is my big chance at sonny-boy. I may never get another."

"You mean it's your big chance at the fortune sonny-boy's slated to come in to."

"Sonny-boy *and* his dough. Look, Dave, I know how you feel about me, but I'm nowhere near as bad as you think I am. Of course Mercedes's money has a lot to do with it. I wouldn't marry Andy if he wasn't coming in to it. But I'm really fond of the kid; I intend to be a good wife; maybe even make a man of him. The big laugh in this thing is that I'll probably turn out the best goddam daughter-in-law Mercedes Cabbott could possibly want for her precious Andrew. End of speech."

She swirled about and yanked the closet door open and walked in and snapped the closet light on. She began to rummage among the garment bags and hangers.

"I know darned well I left my white linen here . . ."

Sandra Jean tilted her head thoughtfully.

150

Tully felt a pang, a stab of recognition. The head-tilt was one of the mannerisms he so loved in Ruth.

He stood there watching the girl. The dim light in the closet played tricks on him. Of course, the hair was different. But if it were darkened to auburn . . . yes, with auburn hair . . .

Something cracked in Tully's head.

Split it wide open.

For an instant he felt dizzy.

He steadied himself in the bedroom doorway.

"Sandra." He had trouble with his voice.

"Yes?"

"The natural color of your hair. It's auburn, isn't it?"

Busy going through the garments in the closet, Sandra Jean made a vague affirmative sound.

He began a slow crossing of the room. It was as if he were wading in an undertow. "Two summers ago. In June. Your hair was its natural auburn then, wasn't it?"

"How should I know? Why on earth — ?"

She whirled. He was just outside the closet, breathing in heavy gusts, making slow grinding sounds with his teeth. She paled and shrank against Ruth's clothes.

"What's the matter with you?" his wife's

sister asked. Her voice was high-pitched suddenly.

Later, Tully was to marvel at his control. All he was conscious of now was the throbbing in his temples and the tickle of sweat as it crept down his nose.

He said thickly, "How long have you known Cranny Cox, Sandra?"

12

Sandra Jean shrank deeper into her sister's clothes closet. "I don't know what you're talking about."

"When did you first meet Cox?"

"I'll let the white dress go for now," she whispered. "I can get it after Andy and I get back."

She made as if to leave the closet. Tully loomed over her. She stopped. Her face was yellow-white now.

"Davey, please. I want to go to Andy."

"Tell me."

"Dave! Let me out of here! Or I'll —"

"What?" David Tully said. "Call Andy? Go ahead. You can tell both of us all about you and Cox. Or yell copper and save me the trouble."

He could see the girl's natural shrewdness take over little by little. She was weighing the probabilities even before the panic was fought down. She smiled up at him.

"I don't know what you're talking about, Dave. You scared me, that's all. You must be out of your mind. Let me pass, will you?"

"Sure," Tully said, stepping aside. She slipped quickly by him. "But I don't think you'll want to go just yet, Sandra. Even if it's only to indulge me a few minutes longer. Don't you want to hear my brainstorm?" She'll have to stay and listen, he thought, if only to find out how much I've guessed.

He was right. Sandra Jean shrugged and said, "Why not?" and sat down at Ruth's vanity, crossing her legs and looking at herself in the mirror. She began to poke at her hair. "But make it snappy, lover, or Andy'll think you've got evil designs on his bride."

"The resemblance," Tully said. "It's been right here all the time, under my nose, and I didn't see how it answered the question."

"What question?" the girl asked, still plumping up her hair.

"The question of how a woman of Ruth's taste and character could foul herself up with a mucking gigolo like Cox. The answer obviously was that she couldn't. So it had to be you, Sandra. You and Ruth are such look-alikes it hits me every time I see you."

"I suppose there is a resemblance," Sandra Jean said carelessly, "and I can see how you'd figure me for more of a tramp than my beloved sister, but aren't you forgetting something, Davey?" Her eyes in the mirror were watchful.

"No," Tully said, "I'm forgetting nothing, Sandra. You mean the fact that when you were indulging in your nasty little peccadilloes you did it using Ruth's name. I wonder why. To protect yourself? Hiding behind your sister's name would do it, all right. Maybe it had a deeper meaning —"

"Such as, Doctor?" the girl laughed. "As long as we're hallucinating . . ." Her eyes kept giving her away.

"Such as that you've always hated Ruth for being what you couldn't be, and by masquerading under her name in a filthy affair you transferred the filth to her in some perverted kind of way." He shrugged. "The psychiatrists can dig into that. What interests me is that it's the only explanation that makes sense."

Sandra Jean began to search among Ruth's lipsticks for the shade she wanted. "For what?"

"For Wilton Lake, for instance," Tully said. Her hand paused for the slightest instant over a lipstick. Then it resumed its motion and she was applying it to her pouting lips. "That was you up at the

Lodge two years ago, Sandra, wasn't it? With Cox? You using Ruth's name and wallowing in a three-day orgy the people up there still remember! That resemblance worked overtime for you, Sandra. I showed one of the maids a photo of Ruth and she said, yes, that was the woman with Cox that summer. It was an honest mistake — seeing a wallet-sized snapshot after the passage of two years, the woman made a logical identification. But I think if we darken your hair and take you up to the Lodge for the old gal to inspect in the flesh . . ."

This time fear flickered in those depths. She set the lipstick down, white-faced again. Tully pressed on remorselessly.

"I don't know why even you took up with a creep like Cox — for the kicks, I guess, rolling around in the gutter to see what it tasted like — but you must have come to your senses, probably gave him some money, and thought you were rid of him. Only it didn't work out that way, Sandra, did it?"

The full lips were drying. Her tongue stole out to wet them.

"Cox wasn't rid of *you*. For some time he let you alone. But then he got sick, and he was broke, and he rummaged around in his dirty little bag of tricks and came up with that weekend. He got in touch with you. And you wrote him a letter — that unsigned typewritten note the police found in his effects: 'Cranny — You keep away from me, and I mean it. What happened between us is ancient history . . . I've found myself a leading citizen here who's very much interested in me and I think he's going to ask me to marry him . . .' That wasn't Ruth referring to me. That was you referring to Andrew Gordon."

He saw her thighs tighten and her rump begin to lift. But then she sank down again.

"You must have scared him off for the time being. Or he was too sick to follow it up. But under Maudie Blake's fat and tender hands he got back on his feet. And he made straight for this town like bad news. And phoned here, asking for Ruth. Andy himself told me that; he took the call when you and he were here and Ruth happened to be out. *Even Cox thought your name was Ruth.*"

Her eyes were darting about now like trapped fish. Tully knew what she was thinking. Not about Ruth. Not about him, or even herself. She was thinking of Mercedes Cabbott's money, and how it was slipping though her fingers.

"That's when you got your big idea, Sandra. You've always had the key to this house. You lifted my gun and went to the Hobby Motel. It was you the Blake woman heard Cox call Ruth. It was you who shot Cox to death."

He could actually see her thoughts snap back to the present. Her head jerked up and she said, "What did you say?"

"I said you murdered Cox."

He thought she was going to faint, and he found himself becoming irritated. Sandra Jean Ainsworth wasn't the fainting type. She was play-acting. Or was she? To hell with her, he thought impatiently.

"Well?"

She shook her head, seemed to be making a great effort. Finally she swallowed, and her lips parted, and her voice cracked as she spoke. "No. No, Davey. It wasn't me."

"You expect me to believe that?" Tully growled. "What do you take me for, a stupid sucker like that oaf in there?"

"Davey, no, no." She got to her feet and went to the bedroom window. She turned to face him, resting her palms on the sill, leaning back so that the curtain framed her head. "This time I'm telling the truth. You've left me no choice."

Tully laughed. "You admit the Wilton Lake shack-up?"

Her head moved ever so slightly.

"You admit typing that note?"

Again.

"You admit stealing my gun? Using Ruth's name? You admit the whole damn thing and expect me to believe you didn't shoot him?"

"I didn't," Sandra Jean said. It sounded real.

Tully was confused again. He sat down on the big bed — *it was king-size, made to order, built especially long, and how tiny Ruth always looked in it and how he used to tease her about it* — just sat there, arms dangling, suddenly without strength or stamina, staring into the past . . . or the future.

"I didn't," a husky voice said in his ear; and he felt the humid tickle of Sandra Jean's breath and the pressure of her body against his back. She had crawled across the bed from the opposite side and seized him softly, like a hostage.

Tully rose violently. The girl fell over backwards with a cry of surprise and pain, exposing her thighs. He reached over and yanked her skirt down so hard the hem ripped.

"Let's keep this clean, you little whore,"

he said through his teeth. He leaned over the girl, and she scrambled away like a terrified bug, tumbling off the other side of the bed and staring up at him from her knees. "I'm not taking your word for anything, understand me, Sandra? Anything! Not after the vicious deal you've given Ruth."

"Yes, Davey," Sandra Jean whispered.

"You say you didn't shoot Cox —"

"No," she whispered, "no."

"Then who did?"

"I don't know."

"But you admit you were there that night with my gun."

"Yes . . ."

"Why? Why my gun?"

She began to whimper. "I didn't know where else to get one. Davey, I swear that's the only reason —"

"Never mind the swearing bit; it doesn't impress me. If you didn't shoot Cox, why did you take the gun in the first place?" He hardly recognized his own voice now; it was harsh and low, without mercy or humanity. "Answer me!"

She clutched the bed. "To scare him. I wanted to scare him."

"And you say you didn't use the gun?"

"I couldn't, Davey. I was too afraid. He

. . . he took the gun away from me. We had a wrestling match over it."

Tully leaned his fists on the bed and glared down at her. "Why did you want to scare him? What was he after?"

"I didn't know when I went there, but I knew Cranny Cox." Sandra Jean's body shook in the slightest shudder. "He was a monster. But a smart monster. I was an idiot to write him about my chance to marry a wealthy man. I might have known he'd try to cash in on it."

"How? By blackmailing you on the strength of those three days at the Lodge? Threatening to tell your husband-to-be about it and so spoil your marriage plans unless you paid up?"

"That's what I thought. But when I accused him of that, he laughed and said he'd hardly break the egg of the golden goose before it hatched. He even offered me a drink and wished me luck with my fiancé."

Tully slowly straightened. It made sense. Why should Cox milk Sandra Jean's modest trust-fund when, by waiting for her to marry a rich man, he would have a fortune to squeeze?

"All right," Tully said.

The girl scrambled to her feet, started to leave.

"All right so far," Tully said, and she stopped in her tracks. "I'm not through with you. So that's all Cox wanted you for, eh? To prepare you for the blackmail to come?"

"Yes, Davey," Sandra Jean breathed. Her eyes were full of fear again.

"And you just walked out of his motel room — leaving my gun behind? Wasn't that a little careless of you, Sandra?"

"You don't understand," she said quickly. "He'd taken it from me and he wouldn't give it back. I wanted it back — I asked him for it. He laughed and said he was keeping it as a memento. I suppose he was afraid I'd change my mind and shoot him after all if he let me get my hands on it again."

Tully brooded.

The girl watched him with anxiety. She took a tentative step toward the bedroom door, stopped as he stirred.

He looked up. "Then what happened to Ruth?"

"I don't know." Her voice rose. "Davey, I don't!"

"Did you see her that night?"

"No —"

"At any time?"

"No, Davey, no."

"You have no explanation for Ruth's disappearance, then? It's simply a great big mystery to you. Right?"

"Yes, Davey. I'm telling you the truth!"

"Sandra." The word had a flat, almost mechanical, timbre. His eyes, sooty with fatigue, stared at her out of a face as rigid as a cheap Hallowe'en mask. "If I find out that you know anything about Ruth's movements that night — where she went — what happened to her — where she is — anything! — I'll kill you. I'll give you one more chance. Where is Ruth?"

She said hoarsely, "I don't know."

For a long time they stood that way.

Then Sandra Jean stirred cautiously.

"Davey. . . ."

"What?"

"May I . . . go now?"

"Go?" Tully looked up. "Go where?"

"To Andy. Remember we had plans to — ?"

He stared at her again, shook his head. "You baffle me, Sandra, you really do. There's only one place you're going, and only one man you're going there with — that's to the police, with me."

"I suppose I have to," Sandra Jean said after a while.

"You have to."

"It means postponing our elopement . . ."

Tully said nothing. The girl became reflective. Watching her, Tully marveled at her resiliency. The fear of the immediate past was gone. The trip to the police was an accepted fact. The problem now was apparently how to mend her fences with Andrew Gordon.

She looked up. Problem solved.

"Will you give me a few minutes with Andy?"

He shrugged.

She went to the living room. Tully followed her as far as the hall. He saw her stoop over Mercedes Cabbott's son, who was asleep, kiss him lightly on the forehead, slip into his lap, begin to murmur into his ear.

Sickened, Tully turned away.

A quarter of an hour later he heard Andy Gordon leave. Tully went into the living room.

"Success?"

Sandra Jean was smoking a cigarette in perfect calm. "I think so. He wasn't as miffed as I expected."

"Maybe Andy's not so keen on this connubial connection as he pretends to be."

"Don't be an ass. His tongue is hanging out."

"How much did you tell him?"

"Just enough. I said something'd come up about Ruth's trouble that couldn't wait, and we'd have to elope some other time."

"Just like that. And he fell for it?"

She smiled. "I gave him a Sandra Special before he could think about it. It's a type of kiss I'm thinking of patenting. It produces amnesia."

Tully did not change expression. "Did you tell him you went to see Crandall Cox on the night of the murder?"

"Of course," Sandra Jean said. "I couldn't have him hearing it from another source, could I?"

"What reason did you give Andy for the visit?"

She said hurriedly, "Oh, something or other that wouldn't disturb his dear addled brain too much. Shall we go, Davey?"

He knew then that Sandra Jean had probably ascribed the visit to sisterly duty, something that involved Ruth as the principal — a total and shameless lie. Tully shrugged and went to the door. So long as Sandra set the record on Ruth straight with the police, he didn't care how she bamboozled Andy Gordon and Mercedes Cabbott. They would have to watch out for themselves.

Julian Smith kept them waiting fifteen minutes.

"Sorry," he said, rising from his desk. He offered no explanation for the delay. He looked quickly from Sandra Jean to Tully and back again. "Hello, Miss Ainsworth."

"Hi, Lieutenant." They had a slight acquaintance.

"What's up, Dave?" Smith said. "Something on Ruth?"

"In a negative sort of way," Tully said. "May we sit down, Julian?"

"Oh! Please." When they were seated Smith said, "I didn't get that, Dave."

Tully glanced at his sister-in-law. "How do you want it, Sandra? You or me?"

"I'm quite capable of speaking for myself." She seemed so self-possessed Tully's glance sharpened. Julian Smith noted his reaction, slight as it was, and became intent. "I wish to make a statement, Lieutenant. Isn't that the way it's put?"

"Statement about what, Miss Ainsworth?"

Sandra Jean ignored the question. Sitting straight-backed, knees primly together, she took inventory of the Homicide man's office. "Exactly how is it done, Lieutenant Smith? Do you have a stenographer in, or is it taken down on tape?"

Julian Smith said gently, "Don't worry your head about the mechanics of my job, Miss Ainsworth. First tell me what's on your mind. You can always repeat it for the official record."

"Stop stalling, Sandra," Tully said. He knew Smith already had the tape recorder going.

She pouted. But then she folded her hands in her lap and stared down at them. "Ruth wasn't the woman who spent those three days at the Wilton Lake Lodge with Cranny Cox two summers ago. I was the one, using Ruth's name."

Tully was watching the detective's face. It gave no sign of surprise.

"What made you decide to come in with this information, Miss Ainsworth?"

"Well, I've naturally been scared to get involved," Sandra Jean murmured. "But my brother-in-law's convinced me it's the only right and decent thing to do. I mean Ruth's being my sister and all."

Julian Smith swung about. "How did you find out about this, Dave?"

Tully was angry. Great expectations, he thought bitterly. "You don't seem impressed, Julian."

"Would you mind answering my question?"

167

"I'll answer your damn question," Tully growled. "I found out about it the same way you should have — I figured it out. Ruth and Sandra Jean look a lot alike. It's a couple of years since the people at the Lodge saw the woman with Cox. Ruth isn't capable of a hot-pillow romance with a cheap woman-chasing crook like Cox. So it must have been Sandra Jean. Q.E.D. Simple?"

"Too simple, Dave."

Tully jumped to his feet. "It's the truth!"

"Maybe," Julian Smith said. "And maybe it's a cook-up between you and Miss Ainsworth to cover for your wife and her sister."

13

David Tully cooled off very suddenly — his urge to grab Smith by the neck and shake sense into him died at birth. He had caught a certain look in Sandra Jean's eye, a look of calculation. She was the problem, not Smith. It was dawning on her that the lieutenant's skepticism gave her a possible out even now.

Tully said very quietly to the girl, "If you have any idea of putting on an act for Julian's benefit and finally 'admitting' that you and I hatched up a cock-and-bull story to save Ruth — forget it, Sandra. This is something that can be proved by having Dalrymple and the maid identify you."

"Sit down, Dave," Julian Smith said.

"Sure."

Tully sat down, his stare pinning Sandra Jean to the wall. He could almost see the computer inside her pretty head whirring and clicking to produce the decision.

It was made. Sandra Jean looked bewildered and hurt. "I don't know why you'd say a thing like that, Davey. I'm telling the truth, Lieutenant. I was the one. And, as

Dave says, all you have to do to prove it is take me up to the Lodge for a positive identification."

"All right," Smith said. "Let's take it from there. Why did you use your sister's name?"

Sandra Jean said coolly, "Dave has a theory that it's because I've always hated her. It's nothing as Freudian as that. I was eighteen, I thought I was being terribly sophisticated, and since I never expected the story to get out I thought using Ruth's name was a good joke. Now, of course, I see what a bad joke it was."

"So when Cox came to town to blackmail Ruth, it was you he really meant?"

"Obviously. He asked me to come over to his room at the Hobby Motel —"

"The night he was shot?"

"Yes. I went."

"Alone? Or with your sister?"

"As far as I know, Ruth didn't know a thing about it. I went alone, yes."

"With the gun?"

"Yes. I took it from Dave's house. I knew it was there. I've always come and gone in the place as if it were my own home."

"Miss Ainsworth, do you realize the implications of what you're saying?"

"I'm not implying anything," she said. "You're inferring."

He blinked at her, sat forward. "Cox tried to blackmail you, and you used the gun?"

"I did not use the gun. Anyway, he took it from me and wouldn't give it back."

Smith knuckled his jaw. "You did intend to use the gun, however?"

Sandra Jean said calmly, "If I'd intended to shoot Cox, I'd hardly have carried a gun traceable to a member of my family. And I'd certainly have picked a better scene for my crime than a wide-open motel on a busy night. I'd have chosen a safer time, place and weapon, Lieutenant, believe me. I took Dave's gun simply to scare Cox."

The detective's face told nothing. "And did you scare Cox?"

She shrugged. "I guess so. He took a crazy chance and jumped me. He didn't know I couldn't have pulled the trigger even if I'd wanted to. Anyway, he wouldn't give it back to me."

"Then your story is that you didn't shoot Cox."

"It's not a story, Lieutenant. It's a fact."

Smith drummed on his desk. "Tell me, Miss Ainsworth," he said suddenly. "What was Cox asking of you?"

"Nothing."

"Come again?"

"Nothing then." Sandra Jean lowered

her head again, modestly. "He knew Andrew Gordon and I were — are . . . well, in love. He was setting me up for a richer haul — after I became Mrs. Gordon." She looked up with a show of anxiety. "I do hope this is all — I mean, confidential, Lieutenant."

"Confidential!" Julian Smith sprang to his feet. "What is this, Dave? Doesn't this girl understand the position she's in? Confidential, she says! Miss Ainsworth, don't you realize that, simply on the strength of what you've already confessed, I have grounds for holding you?"

She smiled.

Smith abruptly sat down again. "There's something cross-eyed about this," he complained. Tully had never seen him so upset. He was beginning to feel queasy himself. She had something up her sleeve, but what? I should have known, he thought. She came along too damn meekly!

"You could hold me, perhaps," Sandra Jean said, "but it wouldn't be for long. Cranny Cox was alive when I left him."

"There's only your word for that," Smith snapped.

"Not at all. I can prove it. Or . . . yes, Lieutenant," she said in the sweetest of voices, "I think I'll let you prove it for me."

"Prove that Cox was alive when you left him?"

"Mm-hm." The girl tugged at her skirt. "Oh, dear, I seem to have ripped my hem somewhere . . . You see, Lieutenant, although I went to the Hobby in a cab, I had the man let me out blocks and blocks from the motel and walked the rest of the way. But when I left, I took a taxi right outside the motel. Cranny took me out to the road and actually hailed it for me — handed me into it, in fact, like the gentleman he wasn't. I was all dressed up and I looked like a lady, if I do say so myself. Taxis don't pick up many ladies outside the Hobby, so I'm sure the cabbie will remember me — and Cranny Cox being so gallant and, of course, alive. In fact, I can even give you a description of the taxi man. He was white-haired, about fifty-five years old . . ."

Tully scarcely heard her rattle on, as Julian Smith scribbled furious notes. The cold-blooded little bitch, he thought. She hadn't said a word to him about that!

"Of course," the detective was saying frostily, "even if this checks out, Miss Ainsworth —"

"Oh, it will check out all right, Lieutenant," she smiled.

"— it could mean that you made a deliberate attempt to establish your departure at a time when Cox was seen alive, only to slip back to the motel later and do the shooting. In other words, a phony alibi."

"I suppose it could mean that," Sandra Jean murmured, "only 'could mean' doesn't carry much weight as evidence, Lieutenant, does it? Anyway, my alibi's a lot better than *that*. If you'll find that taxi driver, I'm sure he'll tell you where he took me, and when. He drove me to an all-night party I'd been invited to in the Heights. People named Bangsworth. And there must have been a dozen people there I knew who'll account for every minute of my time. So, you see, Lieutenant, I simply couldn't have shot Cranny Cox."

Tully could only sit there, numb.

Julian Smith sat there, too. He said slowly, "A few minutes ago, Miss Ainsworth, you told me that Cox asked you to visit him at the motel the night he was shot. Just how did he ask you?"

Sandra Jean's brow wrinkled ever so little. "I don't think I understand, Lieutenant."

"I mean, did he write you? Did he phone you?"

"He phoned me."

"Where?"

"At the Cabbotts', where I've been staying."

Smith leaned forward. "But you said he thought your name was Ruth. How could he have looked for Ruth in a place where you're known as Sandra Jean?"

"Oh, that," Sandra Jean said. "Didn't I explain that? Between the time Cranny came to town and the time he phoned me, he did some snooping. That's how he found out my real name and where I was staying, he said."

The unutterable trull. She hadn't told him that, either.

Tully shut his eyes. Andy Gordon had placed Cox's call to the Tully home, when the blackmailer had asked for Ruth, as having come two days before his murder. So at that time Cox must still have been ignorant of Sandra Jean's real name. In those two days, then, Cox had done his homework. But if by the time of his phone call to the Cabbott house he had known that "Ruth" was really Sandra Jean, why had he . . . ?

Tully heard scraping chairs. He opened his eyes. Smith and Sandra Jean were on their feet.

"But where are you taking me, Lieutenant?" Sandra Jean was saying, not entirely without alarm.

175

"On a tour of the cab companies," the detective said, "to make an honest woman of you. Dave, this won't take too long. Though you don't have to wait if you have something else to do."

Tully shook his head. Julian Smith opened his office door and stood aside, and Sandra Jean swept by in rather a hurry, Tully thought, noting that she was careful not to look at him. He could wait. There were only three or four cab companies in town; it wouldn't take long.

It didn't. Barely an hour later Julian Smith marched back into the office. He was alone.

"Where's Sandra Jean?" Tully got to his feet.

Smith homed in on his desk. "She gave me a message for you. 'Tell my darling brother-in-law he needn't wait for me. I'll hop a cab — I have things to do in a rush.' The last I saw, she was streaking for a phone booth. That's quite a sister-in-law you have."

"So her story is true," Tully said slowly.

The detective shrugged and sat down. "The alibi checks. I found the hack the first cab company I hit. He identified her, all right, and corroborated her statement that Cox put her into the cab that night.

His trip-sheet in the office checks out for time, too. He described Cox to a *T*. For the record I had him hustled over to the funeral parlor for a look at the body, and I just had a call that he made a positive identification.

"And he did take the girl right from the Hobby to the Bangsworths' at the Heights, as she claims. I phoned Mrs. Bangsworth and she gives the girl a clean bill. I also phoned three of the people at the party who Sandra Jean said could testify that she hadn't left the house after she got there, and they so testify — the party didn't break up until five A.M., long past the time of the shooting. One of my men is running down the whole list the girl's given me, but that's just going through the motions. There's no question that Cox was alive when she left him at the motel, and she's alibied for every minute after that. She's absolutely in the clear, Dave. Didn't you know that when you brought her in here?"

Tully said, "No," and had to clear his throat. The detective looked at him curiously. "Where does this leave Ruth?"

"You tell me."

"Well, for one thing, Julian, at least now you know it wasn't Ruth who took my gun to the motel."

"There's still that business of the name."

"Name?"

"The name Maudie Blake said she overheard Cox use that night in addressing his visitor — or one of them. According to Sandra Jean, Cox knew well in advance of the visit or visits that her name was really Sandra Jean. So if that night he called some woman Ruth . . ."

Tully bit his lip. He had foolishly hoped that detail would somehow be lost in the shuffle. "That's assuming Sandra told the truth about what went on in the room, Julian."

"Her alibi story checks to the letter. We have to assume the rest of her story is true, too."

"But that means you think my wife came to Cox's room after Sandra left! How do you know she hadn't come and gone — assuming she was there at all — before Sandra even got there?"

Julian Smith said, "We have the Blake woman's sworn statement as to the time she heard the name Ruth mentioned by Cox in direct address. That time was well past the time we know Miss Ainsworth left. I'm sorry, Dave."

So the Blake woman had lied to him about not remembering the time, too!

Tully was striding up and down the office like a prisoner in a cell. "That sworn statement of Maudie Blake's. She's dead, Julian. It seems to me that if it came to a trial —"

"The admissibility of evidence is a matter for the judge and the lawyers, Dave. I can only do my part of the job."

"You've had your case blown right out of your hands!" Tully cried. "Why do you keep persecuting my wife?"

"Because of that name," the lieutenant said doggedly. "Because she's run away. And it's not persecution, Dave; you know better than that. In the light of those two facts I've got to keep after her. You know that, too."

"But you don't even have a motive any more! Not with Sandra's admission that she was the one who spent those three days at the Lodge with Cox."

"I don't have a motive I can prove yet, Dave, that's true." Julian Smith shook his head in distaste. "You make me say it. Ruth did go to Cox's motel. That makes it pretty hard to avoid the conclusion that she knew him. Well, Cox's relationships with women were strictly one thing. So I've got to work on the premise that not only your sister-in-law but your wife, too, was one of his ex-affairs —"

"No!" Tully's face was purple. "No!" His fist came down with a crash on the Homicide man's desk. *"No, no, no!"* His fist kept smashing at the desk impotently.

Smith said nothing more, letting him rage.

After a while, Tully stopped. A choked sound came out of his convulsed throat, and he turned on his heel and strode out of Smith's office.

David Tully paused on the front steps of the municipal building to gulp the fresher air in mouthfuls and work himself back to some semblance of self-control.

He couldn't blame Julian Smith. Julian wasn't emotionally involved with Ruth. He had liked her (although now that he thought of it, Tully recalled that Ruth had always seemed to have reservations about Julian. Was it because she *was* concealing something unsavory about her past, and a policeman made her uncomfortable?). But he had to be a policeman first and a social being second. Julian had no choice.

His rage, Tully knew, had been directed not toward the Homicide man but to himself. He thought he had made peace with his love and faith; now he found himself doubting all over again.

As he stood there inhaling and exhaling, watching and not seeing the traffic go by, he found a thought pushing itself into the forefront of his consciousness. He tried to push it back; it would not stay pushed back.

If . . . *if* Ruth had had an affair with Cox, surely he knew all along that she *was* Ruth and that Sandra Jean *was* Sandra Jean? But the evidence seemed to indicate that Cox didn't become aware of Sandra's masquerade until a day or so before his death. Then the *if* was wrong. Cox didn't know Ruth. He hadn't known Ruth! . . . Unless . . .

Unless he had originally known Ruth under some other name entirely.

It was possible.

If Ruth could be pictured as having somehow got herself to accept Cox's lovemaking in some remote and hardly imaginable past, she could also be pictured — being Ruth after all — as having done so under a false name. It was more than possible. *If* and *possible* and *false* . . . Tully rested his forehead against the cool stone of the municipal building as his thoughts shattered into pieces that went flying off in all directions.

He started at a touch on his arm.

"Mr. Tully, you feeling all right?" It was

a policeman in uniform, without a hat.

"Yes. Sure, Officer. I'm just going." Tully straightened up.

"I came out looking for you. The lieutenant said you'd just left. There's a phone call for you."

"Here?" Who could that be? "Where, Officer?"

"I'll show you."

He followed the policeman back into the building. There was a table behind the desk sergeant's wicket.

"You can take it here, Mr. Tully. I'll switch you in." The uniformed man sat down at the police switchboard. He said, "Just a minute, ma'am," and plugged in.

Tully thought, Ma'am?

He picked up the phone on the table. "This is David Tully. Who — ?"

"Dave! Norma Hurst." It came into his ear all breathy, as if she had been running.

Tully became alert. "Norma? Something wrong?"

"I'm not sure. Mercedes Cabbott called. Ollie was out . . . She wanted Ollie . . . It was really you she wanted. She called trying to locate you." Her sentences tumbled out. Was she having one of her spells again?

"Yes, Norma?" He forced himself to sound untroubled.

"I called all over trying to find you. Then I thought of Police Headquarters. Have they any news of Ruth yet?"

"Not yet, Norma."

"They're listening to us, of course. Aren't they, Dave? I know they are. Can you come over here?"

"Well —"

"Wait, I think I heard Ollie's car. I'll tell him you're coming over."

"Norma . . ."

But she had hung up.

Ollie answered the door. The bald lawyer looked tired and preoccupied.

"Oh, Dave, come in. Norma says she caught you at Police Headquarters."

Tully nodded. He stepped into the Hursts' living room and said, "What's all this about Mercedes trying to locate me? What does she want?"

"She wouldn't say. Just said for me to find you and bring you to her place."

"Ollieeeee?" Norma's thin voice cut through the house. "Is that Dave?"

She burst into the living room with the power of a tornado-driven straw. Tully was shocked by her appearance. She wore a wrinkled dress. Her lank hair was uncombed. Her features seemed to have

183

been honed to cutting edges overnight. Her eyes . . .

This was a bad one.

Tully kept himself from staring at her. And at Ollie. At times like this, Ollie went through his own brand of hell.

Norma's nails dug into Tully's hand. "Dave, you must hurry. You must find her quickly."

"Yes, Norma. We'll find her. Now stop worrying."

Ollie slipped his arm about Norma's thin shoulders. "You know we'll do our best, hon. Haven't I told you?"

She collapsed against her husband suddenly. "Mercedes will help you, Dave. She loves Ruth like a daughter. That's why she called. I'm sure that's why."

"Maybe it would be better if Ollie stays here with you."

"No, no, I'm fine. I'll be just fine. That's a promise. Ollie has to go with you, help however he can."

From behind his wife's head Ollie nodded slightly.

"Maybe you're right at that, Norma," Tully said.

Outside, Oliver Hurst mumbled, "It's not good, Dave. I had to humor her. Maybe it'll calm her down. I don't dare cross her when she gets like this. Whose car'll we take?"

"Mine," Tully said. Ollie looked out on his feet.

They got into the Imperial and Tully headed it toward the hills.

"I don't know," Ollie said after a while, shaking his head. "For a while there this hassle about Ruth seemed to shake Norma back to her old self. Now . . . She's worse than she's been in months."

"Why don't you try taking her up to the old place, Ollie? The change may do her good."

The "old place" was a Hurstism for an ancient log house some ten miles from town, deep in the foothills that had come down to Norma from her paternal great-grandfather. He had been an early settler, clearing the land, hewing the logs, digging a root-cellar and building the house with his own hands. It had been kept in a good state of preservation, and the Hursts had used it frequently as a weekend woodland retreat in happier days.

But Ollie Hurst shook his head. "It's the one place she mustn't go. Isolation is what she wants, a hole to crawl into. The psychiatrists told me to keep her strictly away from there. They want her to be with people."

"That makes sense, I guess."

"She was after me just this morning to take her up there. Reaction from a dream — a nightmare — she had during the night. Must have been a corker; it took me over an hour to quiet her down."

"Nightmare about what, Ollie?"

"It seems she and Ruth were on a roller coaster. The thing kept going faster and faster. Suddenly a little girl — with no face — was in the middle of the track ahead of them on a tricycle. The roller coaster smashed into her, and the little girl wasn't there any more. Then the coaster shot off the end of the track, tumbling through space, which was full of billions of stars. But it was also pitch-dark. Norma was all alone in just black nothing except stars. Ruth had vanished, too."

And that's a fact, David Tully thought.

14

Ollie Hurst trailed Tully and the butler into the foyer of the Colonial mansion. Tully wondered why the lawyer seemed so uncomfortable.

The two men waited in silence.

Mercedes Cabbott appeared, a fresh-scented and girlish vision in skirt and blouse and delicately thonged sandals. Her white hair was exquisitely coifed, as always; her tiny features and lake-blue eyes were set hard.

She looked Oliver Hurst up and down. "How are you, Ollie?" The words sounded as if she had just taken them out of a deep-freeze.

"I'm still here, Mercedes." To Tully's surprise, the lawyer's tone was just as icy.

"And David." She turned, light-footed. "Shall we go out to the terrace?"

They followed her and the butler out. She indicated two of the white iron chairs. "Would you care for a drink?"

Ollie Hurst said, "No, thank you."

Tully said, "I'll pass, too, Mercedes. I'd

like to get right to your reason for asking me here. I know it wasn't social."

"That's all, Stellers." Mercedes waited until the butler went back into the house. "Perhaps that's best, David. Actually, George has something to say to you, too — he'll be down as soon as he's through changing." Her lips formed a hard line. "What I wanted to talk to you about concerns Andrew. Do you know where he and Sandra Jean are?"

"No," Tully said. What in hell could George Cabbott want to see him about? "But to the best of my knowledge they're planning to elope."

The only sign Mercedes showed was a slight pallor. "So my bluff didn't work. Well, darling, what am I to do?"

"Do?" Tully said. "I haven't any idea." He did not add what he was thinking: And I couldn't care less.

Very suddenly Andrew Gordon's mother turned to Oliver Hurst. "Ollie? Would you have a suggestion?"

Hurst shifted cautiously in his chair. "Are you asking for my professional opinion, Mercedes?"

"You may bill me for it." There was nothing, utterly nothing to be learned from her voice.

"All right," said the lawyer. "Are they of legal age?"

"Yes."

"Then I'll be happy to give you my opinion gratis: There isn't anything you can do about it."

Tully had never heard Oliver Hurst speak in quite that tone. It was composed of notes of bitterness, triumph, regret and barely checked temper; they formed a harsh, uncharacteristic chord. And Mercedes Cabbott's blue eyes glittered like lake ice in deep winter at the sound of it. Whatever lay between the two obviously went back a long, long way.

"I might have expected you to say that," Mercedes said.

"You're licked, Mercedes."

"My dear," the young-old woman said softly, "I'm never licked."

The sun bounced off Hurst's bald head as he shifted violently back to his original position. But he did not reply, preferring to examine the hills in the distance.

Mercedes Cabbott rose and drifted to the edge of her terrace. She stood there gripping the iron railing, her back to the two men.

"It's strange how events influence one another," she said. "One brick falls, and a dozen others tumble after it." She turned to face them, and again her voice was as savagely cold as her eyes. "If Ruth hadn't gone away, Sandra Jean wouldn't have become such a problem. But with Ruth gone, the little slut seizes an opportunity she knows may never recur."

There's no point in my putting my two cents in, Tully thought.

They had forgotten he was there. It was strictly a dialogue.

"You asked me for a suggestion, Mercedes," Oliver Hurst said. The savagery in her voice had, oddly enough, purged him. He sounded almost sympathetic. "I'll oblige."

"Well?"

"For once in your life, acknowledge a defeat. Make the best of this, Mercedes. Try to remember that you're not all-wise and all-powerful, after all."

"Have I ever made any such claims?"

Ollie uttered a faint, incredulous laugh. He shook his head. "Don't you know even now what a tyrant you are? And what a helpless parasite you've made out of your son? Sandra Jean isn't the worst fate that could befall Andy. I think it's even possible she might make a man of him out of the little you've left unspoiled."

She had gone white. Her small hands reached backwards and closed around the railing convulsively.

"You have no right to come into my home and say — !"

"I'm here at your invitation, remember? And I didn't speak until I was spoken to." The lawyer crossed his legs easily. His aplomb seemed to increase in direct ratio to her anger. "However, if you want politeness instead of honest talk, I apologize."

Mercedes sniffed with hauteur and came back to her chair. She seemed actually mollified!

Tully was bewildered. What was it between these two? He had never even suspected anything but a most superficial acquaintanceship. But then he thought, What the hell, it has nothing to do with Ruth; and he shrugged.

The rangy shadow of George Cabbott fell across them. His sun-bleached hair curled damply, as if he had just showered. He wore Bermuda shorts and a sports shirt with the tail out.

Cabbott's eyes, which tended to squint from years of exposure to the sun, widened slightly at the sight of Ollie Hurst. But he merely uttered a pleasant "Hi," stooped over his wife to kiss her — the incongruous thought crossed David Tully's mind of Ferdinand the Bull lowering his massive head to smell a wildflower — and went to the bar-cart near the terrace table. "I take it you gentlemen aren't drinking. Darling?"

"Not just now, George."

"Mind if I have one?"

"What a stupid question for a smart man," Mercedes laughed. The sight of her husband had restored her good humor.

George Cabbott dropped an ice cube into a glass, poured some Scotch in, studying its level critically, then added a few splashes of water from a silver carafe. He joined the group, sitting down and crossing one big blond-felled leg over the other.

"Now, sweetheart, where are we?"

"It's all yours, George." Mercedes gestured helplessly, smiling. "Believe it or not, I haven't the foggiest notion of what George wants to talk to you about, David. When this old bear of mine makes up his mind to do things a certain way, Cleopatra herself couldn't budge him."

"I was told," Cabbott remarked, "to tell you directly, Dave."

"Tell me what?"

Cabbott sipped his Scotch, lowered the glass, agitated it gently. He watched the ice cube slide around. Then he looked up and at Ollie Hurst and said, in a perfectly agreeable voice, "Can you trust this guy, Dave?"

"What?" Tully said, blinking.

"Think nothing of it, Dave," Hurst said. "Nobody trusts a lawyer. Especially on these premises. And especially this lawyer."

"Look, George," Tully said, "I don't know what this is all about, but Ollie Hurst is my friend and my attorney, and anything you may have to say to me you can say in his hearing."

"I don't know," Mercedes's husband said in the same pleasant way. "This might be a special case."

Oliver Hurst gripped the arms of his chair, began to get up. "I think I'd better leave, Dave."

"You sit down," Tully said grimly. "No, Ollie, I mean it! Or I'll leave with you." Hurst sank back. "What's this special-case bit, George? Stop talking like a character in TV."

"If he heard this, Hurst might feel it his professional duty to report it to the police."

"That's a damn nasty thing to say, Cabbott," Ollie Hurst said. He was liver-lipped. "Dave just told you, I'm his attorney. Attorneys don't run to the police to blab about their clients' affairs."

"No offense," Cabbott said with a small smile. "I was given pretty definite instructions."

"Instructions about what, for God's sake?" David Tully cried. "By whom?"

"Ruth."

His head kept swirling like the ice in George Cabbott's glass. The groping thought reached him at last that at some point in recent time he had crossed without noticing it the line between hope and despair. Hope that he might hear from Ruth, that she was even alive . . .

"Alive," he repeated aloud, turning it over on his tongue as if it were a new taste sensation. His voice rose in a joyous shout. "She's alive!"

"Wait a minute, Dave," Ollie Hurst was saying. He had his remarkable eyes fixed on Cabbott.

"Wait for what? George, where is she?" Tully sprang to his feet. "Come on, George, talk, will you?" He grabbed the big man's shoulders and began to shake him.

Cabbott sat quietly, letting himself be shaken.

"David," Mercedes Cabbott said. *"David."*

"What!"

"You'd better sit down and listen. I have a feeling this isn't good news."

Tully sank back in his chair.

"It happened several hours ago, Dave," George Cabbott said. "I began calling all over town for you, and when Mercedes came back home I got her to do some calling, too."

"And wouldn't say a word about why." She leaned over and squeezed her husband's hand.

"I was at Police Headquarters," Tully said. He wet his lips. "George, for God's sake."

"She telephoned me," Cabbott said. "She wouldn't say from where —"

"Did you ask her?" Ollie Hurst asked curtly.

"Of course. She simply refused to say."

"Are you sure it was Ruth?" the lawyer persisted.

"Her voice." Cabbott shrugged. "Unmistakably."

"Could it have been faked?"

"If it was, it was a perfect imitation."

Tully said hoarsely, "Hold it, Ollie. George, if she wanted to get in touch with me, why didn't she do it directly? Why through you?"

"I asked her the same thing, naturally.

She said the police might have your line tapped. Also, she didn't want to chance your talking her out of going away."

"Going . . . away?"

"That's what Ruth said."

"The idiot, the little *idiot*," Mercedes Cabbott said. "Acting noble at a time like this!"

"You mean," David Tully said bleakly, "she's leaving me?"

"I can only tell you what she said, Dave," Cabbott replied in a patient voice. "She said she was sorry for keeping you in the dark so long about her dropping out of sight. She said she was all right physically. She said you wouldn't be hearing from her again until she was safe, perhaps not even then. 'Safe' was her own word, Dave."

"Safe," Tully said. "And she didn't tell you where she was planning to go?"

"No." George Cabbott suddenly drained his glass. "I may as well give you the whole thing, Dave. She said for you to pick up the pieces of your life, and . . . well, she started to cry and said something like, 'Tell Dave he'll always be my sugar-pill,' and then she hung up."

"Her what?"

"Sugar-pill. I take it that's one of her wife-words of endearment? When Mercedes is being especially nice she calls me her hay-bailer."

Ollie Hurst asked, "*Was* that a special word between you and Ruth, Dave?"

"Yes." There was the oddest look on Tully's face. "No imitator would have known about it."

"Then it *was* Ruth." The lawyer abruptly got up. "I think, Cabbott, I'll take one of your drinks after all."

"Help yourself."

"Will you have one, Dave?"

"No. Ollie . . ." Tully got to his feet, too. "I'd like to go now. Make it a quick one, eh?" He crossed the terrace to the doorway, hesitated, turned around. "George."

"Yes, Dave."

"Ruth said nothing at all about Cox? The motel? Anything like that?"

George Cabbott squinted at his empty glass as if it pained him. "That was the last thing I asked her — whether she had shot Cox. That's when she hung up on me. Without answering."

"Thanks, George." Tully walked into the house.

"I'll see you out, David." Mercedes Cabbott rose and hurried after him. Oliver Hurst gulped his drink and followed.

Cabbott remained alone on the terrace, staring into his empty glass.

Mercedes and Hurst caught up with Tully on the front steps.

"David, David, I'm sorry."

"I know," Tully said. Her hand in both of his was trembling and cold. He felt very little himself.

"Sorry for a lot of things," Mercedes Cabbott said; and with some surprise Tully noticed that she was glancing Oliver Hurst's way when she said it. But then she said in the old assured way, "I won't keep you. God bless, David," and she went back into her palace.

The two men walked slowly to Tully's car and got in. "She was talking to you, too, Ollie."

"You noticed that?" And the lawyer was silent. He did not speak again until Tully turned out of the estate into the public road. "I knew her daughter. Kathleen Lavery."

"Oh?"

"Kathleen was a beauty. I was a college kid, and I went head over heels for her. She . . . reciprocated enough to scare Mercedes. I was a nothing, a nobody, without a dime. Mercedes took Kathleen abroad and she was drowned in a boating accident."

"I'm sorry, Ollie."

Hurst shrugged. "It was a long time ago." But Tully noted the gray pallor that had settled over his friend's face.

So now Ollie Hurst had his law practice and his Norma, and Mercedes Cabbott had her Colonial palace to rattle around in and her enigmatic George and her dead — and dying — motherhood.

And I? Tully thought. What do I have?

15

The moment Tully walked into the office Lieutenant Smith said, "There's nothing new." His desk was piled with papers which he rather stealthily covered with a phone book.

"This time you're wrong, Julian." Tully seated himself, uninvited, beside Smith's desk. "You'd better give me a few uninterrupted minutes."

The Homicide man studied him suspiciously. He wore a generally fretful and harassed look today. But then he became relaxed-alert all over; Tully saw it coming over him, like a change of clothing.

The detective picked up his phone and said, "No calls from anybody till I check back," and he hung up and leaned forward on his forearms, clasping his hands. "You've got them, Dave."

"I've heard from Ruth."

Immediately Julian Smith's hands unclasped. He reached for a pencil and pad. "You talked to her yourself?"

"No. It was a message, relayed to me."

"By whom? When?"

"About three-quarters of an hour ago, by George Cabbott. Ollie Hurst was with me. I dropped Ollie off at his home and drove directly here."

"When did Cabbott say he heard from her, and how?"

"Several hours ago. By phone."

"Where was she calling from?"

"She wouldn't say, according to Cabbott."

"Why didn't she get in touch with you in person?"

Tully said wearily, "She thought you might have our wire tapped."

"How sure is Cabbott that it was really her voice?"

"He's positive."

Smith grunted. After a moment he looked up from his pad and said, "Well?" with a trace of impatience. "What was her message?"

"The gist of it was that she was physically okay, that she was going away to some place where she'd be safe, and that I should patch up my life and, presumably, forget her."

"In other words, goodbye Charlie." The detective leaned back in his swivel chair, tapping his chin with the pencil. "Well, Dave, in view of that call, was I right about her, or wrong?"

"Wrong," Tully said. "Wrong, Julian."

"You die hard, don't you?" Smith sighed. "All right, I'll play. How does this prove I'm wrong?"

"How did you ever get to be a lieutenant?" Tully said matter-of-factly. "Don't you realize how convenient that message is for the killer of Cox and the Blake woman?"

"Suppose you spell it out for me!" The detective was a bit pink about the ears.

"If Ruth is never found, the goodbye message nails down the lid on her guilt. The all-points goes out like the ripples made by a stone tossed into a lake. The search gets further and further from town here, the ripples gradually weaken and die away. Goodbye Charlie my foot, Julian! Goodbye case — in the unsolved file."

"You still don't make sense, Dave."

"Look!" Tully's eyes were hard. "The whole thing is damn clear to me now —"

"You mean by guess and by God?"

"I mean by logic and proof!"

"Oh?" Julian Smith said.

"Don't bug me, Julian — listen! Either Ruth took off voluntarily, or she was forced into hiding, abducted. Those are the only two choices, aren't they? If she didn't drop out of sight of her own free will, she's being held somewhere under duress!"

"By the real killer of Cox."

"Yes! From which it follows that Ruth is innocent. No, let me keep going. I'll concede the probability that Ruth did go to the Hobby Motel that night. For purposes of my argument, I don't give a damn whether she went there — as you believe — because she was also one of Cox's ex-romances and blackmail victims or — as I believe — because she'd somehow got wind of Sandra Jean's involvement with Cox and followed Sandra to the motel to protect a wild kid sister. Either way, Ruth's *there,* spying. She sees Cox put Sandra into a cab, go back to his room. But before Ruth can leave, she also sees somebody else call on Cox — and it's my guess it's someone she knew or recognized, or she'd never have hung around . . ."

"Pardon," the detective said. "Your version can be improved. Ruth doesn't just hang around outside after her sister leaves; she follows Cranny Cox into his room and talks to him — whether about herself or about Sandra Jean doesn't matter at this point. There's a knock on the door — the somebody else you set up. Ruth is trapped; she can't get out without being spotted by this mysterious new visitor, so Cox lets her hide in the bathroom.

"Cox lets visitor in. Argument. Visitor picks up your gun — lying on the bed, maybe, where Cox tossed it after taking it away from Sandra Jean. Bang! Cox is dead. Ruth cries out or something — anyway, killer finds her hiding there. So he slugs her and spirits her away. Is that it, Dave?"

"Yes, that's it," Tully said eagerly. "And doesn't it make all kinds of sense? For instance: Why doesn't he shoot Ruth, too? Because he sees that she gives him a heaven-sent out. By smuggling her from the motel and keeping her out of circulation, he makes her the logical suspect for the Cox killing. And she takes the heat off him, or any possibility of it."

"And even then he doesn't kill her," Julian Smith said, nodding, "because he's saving her for the psychological moment. Right, Dave?"

"Right! When he figures the time is ripe, he forces her to make contact with me, to tell me she's going to run as fast and as far as she can, and I'm to forget her."

"And how does he force her to do that?"

"Are you kidding, Julian? By threatening to kill her — or, better still, me. Ruth would certainly knuckle under if she thought my life was in danger!"

"And for this killer that's it, isn't it?" Smith murmured.

"Exactly. He's cinched his frame-up and he has no further need of Ruth. But he obviously can't turn her loose, either." Tully said hoarsely, "Don't you see where this leads to, Julian? *He has to kill her, dispose of her so that no trace will ever be found.* Julian, you've got to forget this nonsense about looking for Ruth as a wanted killer. You've got to concentrate every effort on finding her before she becomes another victim! It may be too late already!"

The lieutenant did not stir.

Tully jumped up, yelling. "My God, Julian, are you a complete moron? Isn't it logical? Doesn't it follow?"

"It follows, all right," Smith said. "The trouble is, it follows from a premise you've cut out of the whole cloth. It's built on unsupported assumption."

"What assumption?" Tully cried. "That Ruth is innocent?"

"The assumption basic to that one, that Ruth is being held against her will and was forced to make the call. What's that assumption rest on but plain air?"

Tully leaned over the desk in a bitter sort of triumph. "I wanted you to put it like that, Julian. It rests not on air but on solid fact!"

"Produce it."

"I haven't a sworn affidavit or an inanimate Exhibit A. I have Ruth's own word. She told me."

"She told you?" Julian Smith said sharply. "Told you what?"

"That the message she asked George Cabbott to pass on to me was a fake."

"Interesting if true. How'd she manage to do that?"

"By slipping in a certain word. It sounded like a harmless term of endearment. It was anything but."

The detective frowned. "I don't get you."

"Haven't you and your wife ever used a secret signal, Julian, a word or phrase with a meaning known only to the two of you?"

"Well . . . yes." The lieutenant looked irritated. "If Gert wants to quit a party early because she's bored or something, she'll mention the O'Toole case to me. There never was an O'Toole case. It's our private code for, 'Let's get out of here.'"

Tully nodded. "With Ruth and me it's sugar-pill."

"Sugar-pill?"

"On our honeymoon Ruth told me about some aunt or somebody, a hypochondriac, who was always running to her doctor with imaginary aches and pains.

He'd give her pills made out of sugar, and she went away happy. For some reason it tickled me, and I promptly christened sugar-pill our secret word for anything imaginary or untrue. If somebody told a supposedly true story, I'd beam at Ruth and call her my little sugar-pill, and she'd understand from that that I knew or thought the guy was lying his head off. Or if we were introduced to somebody, especially a gal, that Ruth thought I was showing too much of an interest in, she'd say sweetly to me, 'Isn't Miss So-and-So fascinating, sugar-pill?' and I'd get the message: My wife thought the gal was a phony."

"So?"

"The last thing Ruth said to George Cabbott before she hung up was, 'Tell Dave he'll always be my sugar-pill.' That was the tipoff, Julian. Ruth was telling me, 'Don't believe a word of what I've said. This is a phony.' It could only mean she was forced to make the call, told what to say. Does that bear out my theory or doesn't it?"

Smith was silent.

Tully kept looking at him, puzzled.

Finally the lieutenant said, "You wouldn't be making this up, Dave, would you?"

He fought a battle with himself, and won. "No, Julian, I wouldn't and I didn't. But if you doubt me, call Cabbott."

"That wouldn't prove anything. I have only your word for it that sugar-pill has a secret meaning — the meaning you claim it has — for you and Mrs. Tully."

Tully shook his head and laughed. "The one thing that didn't occur to me was that you'd doubt my word." He shrugged. "Well, that's the only proof I can give you, Julian. I can't see that you and I are going to have much more to say to each other. I've had it."

He made for the office door.

Lieutenant Smith said, "Wait, wait, will you?"

Tully stopped, waited.

"Damn it all, Dave, this puts me in a real spot. It might mean my job . . ." But then the Homicide man got to his feet, and when he spoke again it was with decision. "If your analysis is right, I'll have to reverse my field. And fast, because Ruth is in for it. Go home and stay out of my hair!"

16

Tully went home.

He let himself into the silent house and sank limply into the big chair in the living room. His legs felt like old rubber and a great lassitude had sucked him dry. How long was it since he had come home from the capital — a day, two days, three? He could not remember.

Julian was right. He could do no more. Now it was in the hands of the police . . . now that they were looking for an innocent woman in danger of being murdered instead of for a murderer.

Funny how this thing, Tully thought, has kept testing my faith in Ruth. Down, up, down, up . . . He laid his head far back and stretched his legs gingerly.

Twilight was coming on and the room was sinking into shadow.

First he had destroyed her image. Then he had resurrected its fragments and put them back together. Now she was to be destroyed in the flesh . . . dead . . .

The shadows deepened into near-darkness. The thought of turning on the lights made him wince. Light meant seeing the things they had bought together, lived in, cherished. Light meant Ruth. Better the black gloom and the silence.

The silence.

The silence?

Noiselessly Tully shifted his position in the chair until he was sitting up, ears cocked, straining. There had been something in the silence that made it not quite silence. A sense of presence . . . With one leap he was out of the chair and across the room, his hand shooting out to the light switch.

He whirled.

Norma Hurst stood in the archway that separated the living room from the rear of the house. She must have been standing there, Tully thought, for a long time — perhaps since he had come home.

He felt the flesh of his forearms gather itself into little eruptions of dread.

This was a Norma Hurst he had never seen before. She had combed her drab hair with great care but the result was curiously fumbling. Her long thin face was grotesque with make-up, as if a small child had tried to imitate her mother's toilet. And her eyes . . . her eyes were not Norma's at all. They were overlarge and underbright; they looked blind.

"Norma," Tully said; he tried to make his voice sound natural, but it came out in a croak. "What are you doing here? How did you get in?" She must have climbed through one of the bedroom windows.

Norma put her forefinger to her wildly rouged lips. "Not so loud," she said. "She'll hear me."

Her voice was strange, too. It had a throb in it, a sort of excitement, that gave it an unpleasantly eerie timbre.

"Who'll hear you, Norma?"

"Mother, of course." He saw her shrink a little, as if she were afraid.

It took all his will-power to go to her, smiling, and take her hand. Her flesh was icy. She resisted his pull.

"You're going to take me to her. She's here, I know she's here. I don't want to see her."

"There's no one here but us, Norma."

"You shouldn't call me that."

"What?" Tully said, bewildered. "Call you what?"

"That name. The name of that flat-chested horror."

"You mean . . . Norma?"

"Please," Norma said sharply. "You know

perfectly well that my name is Kathleen."

She had plunged over the edge.

Tully knew he must reach the telephone, call for help. Ollie? She must have slipped away from him. Ollie was undoubtedly hunting for her right now. The police? No . . . Dr. Suddreth!

Dr. Suddreth was the nearest thing the Tullys had ever had in the way of a family physician. Suddreth was no psychiatrist, but he would do in an emergency. At least control her, know whom to call . . .

Norma had drifted toward the middle of the living room. Her face was twisted with worry. "I can't seem to remember where Ollie introduced us. Was it at the country club dance last week?"

"Why, yes," Tully said, managing a smile. "Oh! Would you excuse me a moment?"

"For what?" she said with sudden sharpness.

"I forgot. I have a call to make."

"No!" she said. "No — phoning — mother." Her lower lip stuck out resentfully.

"Mother?" he repeated mechanically. How was he to get to the phone?

"As if you don't know! Don't try to fool me. You know very well my mother is Mercedes Lavery." She got into a crouch, looking around, whispering. "She's here, isn't she? You're in this with her! And Ollie calls you his best friend! Where is she hiding?" Her glance kept darting about.

"Merce — your mother isn't here," Tully said in a reassuring tone. "And of course I'm Ollie's best friend. Now why don't you sit down and make yourself comfortable while —"

"You are, aren't you?"

"What?"

"Ollie's best friend. Otherwise you wouldn't let us meet here. Mother's made it impossible for us to meet anywhere else."

It was hard to follow the logic of her delusion. The damn phone, so near. But the delusion might be a temporary thing. I can't risk pushing her toward the thin edge of total madness, Tully thought.

She was wandering about the living room now, humming a shapeless little tune. Suddenly she stopped before the bar.

"I want a drink," she said.

"You, Norma — ?" He stopped quickly. Surprise had made him forget. Norma didn't drink.

She was looking at him with mean, hopeless resentment. "I ask you once more to stop calling me that *name*. Do you hear me? Do you?"

"Yes. Yes, of course, Kathleen. Sorry."

"Kathleen. That's my name."

"Kathleen."

He wondered if he dared try force. He might be able to wrap her in a blanket or something and tie her up until Dr. Suddreth arrived. No, he thought, she might tumble right over the edge. The safest thing was to humor her as best he could while he figured out a way to make the phone call without upsetting her.

"I want a drink," Norma Hurst said in exactly the same way as before. As if their interchange betweenwhiles had not taken place at all.

"What would you like . . . Kathleen?"

It pleased her. "Now you remember," she said gayly. "Why, Scotch on the rocks. Make it a double."

Norma asking for a double Scotch!

But then a thought struck Tully.

"Sit down, Kathleen. I've got to get some ice from the kitchen for your drink —" He could phone for help from the kitchen extension.

But Norma said, "No ice, thank you."

"You said on the rocks," he said desperately.

"No ice," she repeated.

He poured a huge slug of Scotch into a

highball glass and handed it to her, hope returning. Norma didn't drink because she couldn't; hard liquor either made her sick or sleepy. In either event . . .

"Thank you," she said, and held the glass without attempting to drink from it.

"Drink up, Kathleen," Tully said heartily. "You asked for a double."

"Oh, yes," she said in a vague way; and she raised the glass and barely wet her lips. Tully turned and poured himself a drink almost as copious.

"Let's go into my den, Kathleen," he said, forcing another smile. "It's comfier there."

Rather to his surprise, she said, "All right," and ambled along in his wake.

He sat her down in his oversized leather chair and hovered over the telephone without seeming to do so. If only someone would call!

"I suppose you've wondered," Norma said brightly — she was sitting in a stiff position that made him wince — "what I can possibly see in a man like Oliver Hurst."

"Well . . . yes."

"I know everybody does. What people don't realize is that the beautiful Kathleen Lavery — they call me that, don't they? — with all this money and position, is way down deep the unhappiest girl in town. The beautiful Mercedes — they call mother that, too, don't they? — doesn't understand that I need to be needed for myself, for what I am inside, not for what I look like and have. Ollie Hurst needs me as a person — the only man I've ever known who does. What do I care what Ollie looks like? Or that he hasn't a dime? He's mad about *me*. And he always will be."

Under other circumstances Tully would have been fascinated. This is how it must have been, he thought, seen through Norma Hurst's eyes.

"You aren't listening," Norma said. She was still sitting rigid on the edge of the chair, still holding the glassful of untouched Scotch.

"Oh, but I am — Kathleen," he said hastily. "Please go on."

"There! You remembered again." She smiled, a painful surface adjustment of muscle tissue. "Why did you keep calling me that other name? You know, that was cruel of you. Poor Norma can't help being what she is."

"I'm sorry," Tully said. Idly he removed the handset from its cradle. "I mean I'm sorry for —"

"*Will* you stop playing with that phone?"

Norma said shrilly. "It makes me nervous." He replaced the handset. "What was I saying? Oh, about Norma. She's so sensitive and high-strung, you know. And *so* unattractive. Of course, she's hopelessly in love with Ollie. The only way she could possibly get him would be to catch him on the rebound while I'm out of the picture. Poor Norma."

So that was it. His skin crawled.

"It may happen, too," Norma said, staring into space over her glass. "That horrible mother of mine! She's offered me a 'compromise.' She's taking me abroad for three months, during which I'm not to see or communicate with Ollie. If I still want him when we get back, mother says, she'll give us our blessing."

"I see," Tully said.

"But I know *her*, the way her mind works. She's figuring on tricking me, the way she always does. Divine Mercedes! If people only *knew* her . . . She'll pretend to be sick, or she'll find some other excuse to keep us in Europe indefinitely. And that will be Norma's chance."

Tully could not help asking, "Then why are you leaving?"

"I have no choice. I'm under age. It's going to be a *battle*. Because I'm going to fight just as hard to talk mother into keeping her word."

"How does Ollie feel about this?"

"Oh, he doesn't know yet. About my going away, I mean. I'll have to tell him soon. The whole story — Where are you going?"

Tully had edged over to the doorway, his mind made up. "To see a man about a dog." It was a phrase, he recalled, popular in Kathleen's day. "Why don't you drink your drink, Kathleen? You've hardly touched it."

She glanced down at the glass with the same vague smile. Tully slipped out of the den. He went quickly into the master bedroom, shut the door without noise, snapped on the light and was over at the night table diving for the telephone book under the bedroom extension in one scrambling leap. Just as he found the *S's* he heard a car turn into his driveway.

By the time Tully managed to leave the bedroom without alarming Norma Hurst and make his way through the rear service door around to the driveway, Ollie Hurst had his ignition and headlights turned off and was coming around the front of his car.

"Ollie."

"Dave, is that you?"

"Yes —"

"Dave, it's happened again —"

"I know."

"She's here?" the lawyer cried.

"Not so loud." He grabbed Ollie's arm. "She's inside. I was just going to call Dr. Suddreth."

"How is she, Dave?"

"Not good."

Oliver Hurst slumped against his car. In the light coming from the bedroom window he looked as if he were going to collapse.

"How far gone is she?"

"She thinks she's Kathleen Lavery."

Ollie was struck dumb. With his head thrust forward and his mouth open and his bald head he looked something like a carp. Then he said, "Kathleen Lavery. Why in God's name . . . ?"

"From what she's been saying, Ollie, I think this goes back a long, long way. Back to her wedding day."

"That was the happiest day of her life!"

"Only on the surface." It was hard for Tully to look at the lawyer. "She's cracked up twice now. Once when little Emmie was killed. Now when Ruth — the best friend Norma ever had — when Ruth's been accused of murder. I'm no expert, Lord knows, but it seems to me this particular gambit began when she married you — when unconsciously she felt that Kathleen's death made her marriage possible. She's carried the load of that guilt around ever since."

"I don't understand," Ollie muttered.

"You'd better start trying," Tully said, more harshly than he intended. "Don't you see how fiercely glad Norma must have felt when Kathleen drowned? But at another level she was shocked at those feelings. I suppose a psychiatrist might say the resulting guilt made it possible for Norma to keep functioning. I don't know — I'm sure it all goes back even further than that. Whatever it is, wherever the hell it stems from, you'd better get her to your psychiatrist fast." Ollie nodded and they hurried toward the service entrance. "Where were you, Ollie?"

"I could see she was working up to something. But I thought she'd be all right if I went for some groceries she mentioned we needed. When I got back from the shopping plaza she was gone. I kept calling around, and hunting for her, till it occurred to me she might have come here. Thinking maybe Ruth was back, or something."

They found Norma in the living room. She was standing at the bar, pouring more Scotch into her glass. It kept slopping over.

She turned and saw her husband and her whole long, taut face screwed up as if she were trying to see through a dense fog.

"Ollie . . . ?"

Hurst's cheeks, gray and slick, twitched as he moved toward her. "Everything's going to be all right," he said nervously. "I'll take you home now, Norma."

She hurled the glass at his head. It sailed past him and smashed against the opposite wall, drenching both men.

"Don't call me that *name!*" Norma screamed. Everything in her face was contorted except her eyes; they remained dull and remote. "It's my mother, isn't it?" she panted. "So she finally got to you, too. She's turned you against me, Ollie. You're all against me!"

"Stop her, Ollie!" Tully shouted.

Hurst was nearer, but her violence had paralyzed him. And Tully was too late. Norma burst through the French doors and disappeared in the darkness of the patio. Tully dashed out after her.

"Ollie, switch on the patio lights!"

The lawyer stumbled to the wall and snapped on the switch. The patio and the grounds beyond lit up like a stage set.

Norma Hurst was crouched under the aluminum awning above the Tullys' field-stone barbecue pit. The long barbecue knife was in her clutch. Bubbles made a froth at the corner of her mouth.

"My God," Ollie Hurst whispered.

"Save your self-pity for some other time," Tully snapped. "We've got to get that knife away from her. You circle to her right. But *slow*."

He drifted toward the left. "Kathleen," he said. "Don't be afraid. No one's going to hurt you. We're here to help you." He kept up the pleasant-toned reassurances, trying to get all her attention. "Why don't you put that thing down? I'd like to talk to you, Kathleen. Kathleen . . . Kathleen . . ."

Ollie Hurst had it almost made. Two steps more . . . He chose that moment to stumble over something in the grass.

As Norma began to whirl, Tully rushed her, grabbed the knife close to the handle, and twisted. To his amazement, the knife refused to come away. Then he felt her other hand clawing at his face and he was fighting for his life.

"Ollie — !" he choked. "Pin her arms!"

Her husband got behind her mechanically, threw his arms about her. She was making blubbering sounds now, like an animal, her teeth glittering in the strong lights. Tully got both hands on the haft of the knife and wrenched. He staggered back as she suddenly released it, lost his balance and fell heavily to the grass. Instead of struggling aimlessly she doubled over and brought her right heel up in a vicious backward kick. Ollie Hurst let out a whooshing *oomph!* and then a yelp and sat down.

She was free.

Gasping, she began to scramble up the slope of hillside beyond the perimeter of the lights. Tully flung the knife as far as he could in the opposite direction and dashed after her, launching himself in a flying tackle. They both fell, face down.

"I'll kill you. I'll kill you," Norma Hurst shrieked. She slithered about in his clutch like a fish, everything going at once, arms, hands, fingernails, legs, feet, teeth.

There was only one thing to do, and Tully did it. He got his right hand free and punched her in the jaw.

17

When the private ambulance drove away
Ollie Hurst, looking eighty years old, got
into his car and began to back out of the
driveway. Tully walked along, one hand on
the driver's door.

"Let me know what the psychiatrist says,
Ollie."

The lawyer swallowed. "Dave . . ."

"Forget it. If you need me, call."

Tully waited at the edge of the road until
Oliver Hurst's car disappeared around the
curve. Then he went into the house and
made for the phone in the den.

"Julian? Dave Tully. I've got to see you."

"What about?" The Homicide man
sounded tired and peevish. "I was just getting set at the TV."

"It's important, Julian. May I come right
over?"

"To my house? My wife's walking around
half-naked. Where you calling from?"

"Home."

"I'll come over there."

Tully hung up and went into the kitchen

224

and dug around in the refrigerator. Nothing but cold cuts. He made a face and set the kettle on to boil. He was just pouring hot water into the big mug with the word PAPA on it when he heard Julian Smith's car pull into the driveway.

He let the detective in and said, "How about a cup of coffee? I know you don't drink."

"Instant?" The detective was in rumpled slacks. He needed a shave.

"That's all there is in the house."

"The hell with it," Smith said.

He followed Tully into the kitchen and sat down wearily. "How'd you get those scratches on your cheek?"

Tully set the kettle back on the electric range and sat down to his coffee. "That's the reason I want to talk to you, Julian. Norma Hurst did that."

"Norma Hurst?" The lieutenant stared at him.

"I found her here when I got home. She's gone off the deep end again, Julian. She thinks she's Kathleen Lavery."

Julian Smith slowly took out a crumpled pack of cigarettes. "Kathleen Lavery . . . She was Mercedes Cabbott's daughter, wasn't she? Died in a boating accident in Europe somewhere?"

"That's right."

Smith looked puzzled. He lit his last cigarette, made a ball of the empty package, glanced around, then stuck the paper ball in his pocket. "What happened, Dave?"

"Ollie went out food-shopping and she took off. I had to handle her with kid gloves, and she did quite a bit of talking — as Kathleen. Finally Ollie got around to looking for her here. She went completely off her rocker and into a violent phase — got hold of my barbecue knife, and I had to knock her out. Delusions of persecution."

"Where is she now?"

"At Pittman, the private sanitarium. Ollie called for an ambulance. That's the place she was in after their child died."

The detective looked around for an ashtray, saw none, and tipped the ash into his cupped hand. "I don't get it, Dave. I'm sorry, of course, for both of them, but why did you have to get me out at this hour of the night to tell me about it?"

"Because I think what happened tonight is tied into the Cox case."

Smith looked around again for an ashtray. "Don't you have an ashtray?" he asked irritably. Tully got up and went into the den and brought back an ashtray. It seemed to make the Homicide man feel better. He emptied his hand of ashes and tapped some more from his cigarette into the tray and said in a good-humored tone, "You sure you aren't the one who's gone off his rocker, Dave?"

"I'm saner than you are, with your damn compulsive neatness," Tully snapped. "Here's what I learned via Norma's delusion tonight: Kathleen Lavery and Ollie Hurst were in love with each other. In fact, they planned to get married. Mercedes characteristically interfered — talked Kathleen into a three-month separation from Ollie in Europe. The whole thing became academic when the girl was drowned in Switzerland."

"So?" the lieutenant asked, unimpressed. "What's that ancient history got to do with this Cox crumb's murder at the Hobby Motel a few nights ago?"

Tully said slowly, "I think Crandall Cox's killing had its origins in that ancient history. He may have come back here to shake down Sandra Jean —"

"And Ruth?"

"Okay, and Ruth! — but his killing had nothing to do with either one of them. *I think Cox was murdered by Kathleen Lavery.*"

Julian Smith blinked. "Are you nuts, Dave, or am I?"

"Listen to me, will you?" Tully said tensely. "Norma's lived all her married life with the guilty knowledge that she got Ollie Hurst only because Kathleen Lavery died. The guilt has built up to the point where apparently Norma feels the compulsion to deny that the girl died at all. But in the real world the girl *is* dead. The only way Norma can resurrect her is to slip into a deluded state and become Kathleen herself.

"Now look!" Tully leaned over the table toward the silent Homicide man. "Cranny Cox was born and brought up in this town. He was a no-good and a girl-chaser from his teens. If you dig deeply enough, Julian, I'm betting you'll find that in those days Cox chased Kathleen Lavery and, what's more, caught her and made time with her.

"Norma knows this —"

"How?"

"How the hell do I know how?" Tully cried. "Maybe Kathleen told Ollie after they fell for each other, and Ollie told Norma when they got married. Anyway, the other day Cox comes back here. Somehow Norma finds out, probably through Ruth. But Norma's already nursing the delusion that she's Kathleen. She goes to see Cox that night — *as*

Kathleen. Cox doesn't realize he's dealing with a mental case, tells her to get lost or something — almost certainly, being Cox, laughs in her face when she calls herself Kathleen. It triggers Norma's violence — I saw it happen tonight. And there's the gun, my gun, within reach. Julian, I tell you the answer to this puzzle is that Norma Hurst shot Cox while she thought she was a girl dead God knows how many years!"

"And your wife?" Julian Smith asked.

"You mean what's happened to her?"

"That's exactly what I mean."

"But don't you see?" Tully cried. "In the grip of that delusion Norma's as strong as a man — and a damn strong man at that! I had to clip her on the chin because I couldn't subdue her any other way, and you know I'm no weakling, Julian. I tell you Norma took Ruth forcibly to some hiding place, maybe tied her up and gagged her. Maybe the doctors can give Norma one of those new drugs they're using on mental patients, find out where Ruth is before she starves to death! I know, Julian, it sounds pretty wild —"

Smith leaned over and touched Tully's hand. "Relax, Dave, or you'll be needing a paddy wagon yourself. I've got a full-scale search going for Ruth on a round-the-clock basis. She'll be found."

"Then you don't buy this Norma-Kathleen theory," Tully said bitterly.

"No, Dave," the lieutenant said.

"Why the hell not!"

"Well, for one thing, that telephone call from Ruth. If she's innocent, the killer forced her to make that call. It's not the kind of behavior a mental case like Norma would evince, from what I know about such cases. It isn't the type of aberration that sets up a pigeon to cover up a killing. If Norma's type of psychopath had done it, she'd probably have shot Ruth on the spot and gone on a rampage and shot at every living thing in sight. I'm sorry, Dave."

Tully sagged in his chair. "So I'm back where I started," he muttered. "There's an out for everybody in this thing but Ruth."

He got up heavily and went to the kitchen window. The house suddenly felt like a prison.

"By the way," Julian Smith's voice said from behind him, "Ruth's picture is being telecast over every TV station in the state tonight. It may help."

"May. Will it?"

"I've seen it happen, Dave. A gas station attendant, a waitress in a diner, a pedestrian on a street corner — we'll get plenty

of calls, and we won't ignore one of them."
Tully felt the detective's hand on his
shoulder. "Why don't you take a pill and
hit the sack? I promise to wake you up per-
sonally if there's any news at all."

"Go to hell," Tully said.

18

After Smith's departure Tully prowled about the house. A new thought had come to plague him, of having recently seen or heard something meaningful. A word, a key, a clue — an open-sesame that with one push would reveal the truth.

But what was it?

He holed up in the den, trying desperately to raise from the dead whatever-it-was. He sat stiff and strained until sweat slicked his forehead. Finally he muttered a curse on all darkness.

Tully heaved himself out of the chair and went to the phone. He dialed Information for the home telephone number of the city editor of the *Times-Call*, Jake Ballinger.

"Dave Tully?" Ballinger was yawning. "Something?"

"Well, for one thing I want to thank you for the way you've handled the Cox story, Jake," Tully said. "I mean as regards my wife."

"We've printed the facts. I left my tabloid techniques back in Chicago." The

232

rumble sounded interested. "What's up, Dave?"

"I need a favor. Will you let me go through your files?"

Ballinger said immediately, "Meet me outside the shop."

A jalopy was parked before the newspaper building when Tully drove up. The bulky newspaperman promptly hopped out. He looked as expectant as an old birddog.

"What's the yarn, Dave? I expect quid for my quo."

"I haven't one — yet."

Ballinger gave Tully a sharp look and led the way into the partly darkened building. The rumble of press machinery was giving the old floors the shakes. Upstairs, a crew of three was still on watch in the newsroom. Locally, the paper was published as the morning *Times* and the afternoon *Call*, with a *Times-Call* appearing on Sundays.

The old man plodded past the newsroom on his flat feet to a glass-partitioned office. He opened the door and snapped on a light. Tiers of laden shelves reached to the ceiling.

"We're running cuts of your wife in the morning edition," Ballinger said. "Headquarters request. I gather the gendarmes of our unfair city don't think Mrs. T.'s so guilty any more. Why, Lieutenant Smith sayeth not. Any news?"

"She's not guilty at all, Jake."

Ballinger kept eyeing him. "This is our morgue. What are you after, Dave?"

"Kathleen Lavery."

"Lavery . . ." Ballinger's hard blue eyes turned inward. "Oh, yes. Why?"

"I'm not sure," Tully said. "I think Cox had other reasons for returning."

"Such as?"

Tully shrugged. "He staked his life on coming back here. He must have had a pretty solid expectation of loot — real loot — to take such a risk."

"And you think it goes back to Kathleen Lavery?"

"I don't know what to think, Jake. This is from desperation. Maybe your files have the answer."

Ballinger rummaged through a card-index file, drew a card out, moved to the shelves. Consulting the card, he fished nearly a dozen small, flat cardboard boxes from the shelves. He opened them one by one and from each took out a round flat tin.

"Let's take these over to the viewer, Dave."

"Microfilm?"

The old newspaperman chuckled. "Unto even a one-horse town cometh technology."

Tully trailed Ballinger to the microfilm viewer. Ballinger turned the projector on and slipped the top film into place. A front page of the *Times* sprang into being on the viewer's frosted plate.

"Watch the heads, Dave. We click from page to page till we hit the story relating to our subject."

For forty-five minutes David Tully watched a beautiful young girl grow up. The Laverys leaving for Europe. The Laverys returning from Europe. Young Miss Kathleen Lavery entertaining with a Christmas party at the country club, under the chaperonage of Mrs. Mercedes Lavery. At fourteen — taking a blue ribbon at the horse show — the budding teenager pictured sitting her sleek mount seemed to Tully a lonely little figure. Swimming on her school team in an intra-state competition. Entering a junior tennis tournament in England. Story after story . . .

And then her death.

"Hold that, Jake."

Ballinger held it, looking curious. Tully skimmed through the story. ". . . vacationing in Switzerland with her mother. Miss Lavery was pronounced dead from accidental drowning after her boat capsized on Lake St. Cyr. Her body was washed up on the lake shore shortly after dawn yesterday morning, Swiss time. It was found by a group of early morning swimmers . . ."

Tully scanned the rest of the file. It concerned the girl's funeral, and a final obit recounting her short history and family connections.

"That's it." Ballinger clicked off the viewer.

Tully mumbled: "No mention of Crandall Cox."

"Why should there be?"

"He preyed on women most of his life, specializing in the upper crust. I thought he might have done a job on the Lavery girl. She was certainly the richest and most vulnerable target in this town."

"He'd have had a pretty tough time," the old newspaperman said dryly, "worming his way into her set, from what it used to be like in those days."

Tully scowled, watching Ballinger stow away the films. "By the way," he said suddenly. "How did Kathleen happen to drown? She was an expert swimmer, according to one of these stories. Or were you still in Chicago at that time, Jake?"

"No, I'd been here about six months when it happened. It was a big story. Anyone or anything connected with Mercedes has always been a big story here." The old man shrugged. "There was a lot of back-of-the-hand talk, because the Swiss authorities didn't come up with any clearcut explanation for the accident. There'd been a squall of sorts, and the girl had taken the boat out alone, presumably — they finally decided that when the boat upset she got a crack on the head, or a cramp. Or swam around in circles in the dark till she was exhausted."

"It doesn't sell me," Tully said.

Jake Ballinger looked at him. "Are you suggesting that the bonnie Kathleen was murdered?"

"How the devil do I know what I'm suggesting?" Tully exploded.

He and Ballinger went down into the street.

"Thanks, Jake."

"For what?" the old editor rumbled.

In spite of himself, David Tully grinned. "For nothing, I guess."

Back at home Tully thought and thought, and finally he resorted to the telephone again. He hesitated only a moment.

Had Sandra Jean already taken Andrew Gordon across a state line to get married? Although that would be pretty fast work even for Sandra Jean . . . He dialed the Cabbott number.

The butler answered.

Tully asked for Mr. Gordon.

Andy came on. "What do *you* want?" His voice was guarded.

"I'm relaying a message from Sandra Jean."

"Not so loud!"

"She wants to meet you here — in my house — right away." He used the most conspiratorial tone he could contrive.

"But I was supposed to meet her at the Blue Iris in a half hour!" The boy sounded in an agony of indecision.

"Look, Junior, I'm simply telling you what Sandra said. I don't give a damn whether you meet her or not."

Tully ended the conversation with a slam. He ran to the picture window and waited.

Twelve minutes later headlights swung into his driveway. Tully had the front door open before Andy could ring.

"Come in, fly," Tully said.

"What?" the boy said blankly.

"I said come in."

Andy Gordon came in. His eyes were bloodshot and his dark young face looked puffy and hung over.

"Where's Sandra Jean?" He looked around suspiciously.

"She isn't here," Tully said.

"What d'ye mean she isn't here?" Andy cried. "You said —"

"I wanted to talk to somebody about Kathleen Lavery," Tully said.

The boy blinked and blinked. "What the hell is this?"

"I decided your stepfather George probably doesn't know, and your mother would be too tough. That leaves you, Andy."

The big muscular young body seemed to swell. "I'm not so tough, is that what you mean?"

"You're not tough at all, Andy."

The boy came at him like a blind bull. Tully sidestepped and hooked hard. Blood spurted from Andy's nose. He hit the floor hard. He grabbed at his nose, looked at his blood-smeared hand with terror, and began to cry.

"That's more like it, kid," Tully said. "Because the next time you swing on me it'll cost you a mouthful of teeth."

"Damn you!" Andy Gordon wept. "I'll kill you . . ."

"I haven't got the time to let you. I want answers, Andy, and I want them straight and now."

"Answers to *what?*" the boy said viciously.

"It's about Kathleen."

19

"Crandall Cox and Kathleen," Tully said. "Did they know each other?"

"How would I know?"

"She knew Ollie Hurst, even thought of marrying him. She knew Cox too, didn't she?"

"I tell you I don't know! Man oh man, I'll fix you for this, Dave —"

"Stick to the subject at hand. Mercedes took Kathleen abroad to keep her from marrying Ollie. Did Cox figure any way in that?"

"I don't know!"

"You do know," Tully said. "Mercedes runs a pretty taut ship. She's held Kathleen's fate up to you since you were in diapers — I mean, as a horrible example of what comes from crossing mama. Right, Andy?"

Andy was pressing a handkerchief to his nose. "Wait till she hears about *this*."

"I'm not impressed any more," Tully said. "I have a wife to get back. Are you going to talk?"

"The papers —" Andy shrank back.

"I read the papers, Andy. They printed the official handouts. Your half-sister was a good enough swimmer to be on her school swimming team. She didn't drown accidentally, now, did she?"

Andy glared up at him. Whatever it was that he saw in Tully's eyes, it made his own eyes shift.

"No. She didn't."

"Well," said Tully. Then he said, "And she wasn't murdered, either. The Swiss police are among the best in the world. They wouldn't have missed that."

"I don't follow you," the boy said sullenly.

"Kathleen was the daughter of a millionaire American. And there was no proof her death wasn't an accident. Under the circumstances, didn't the Swiss authorities decide to let it go at that?"

"I don't know what you're talking about."

Tully stooped over him and said softly, "Kathleen killed herself, Andy, didn't she? Took that boat out in a squall and deliberately upset it and let herself go under? Probably leaving a suicide note that Mercedes destroyed. Isn't that the truth about Kathleen?"

The boy's voice was little more than a whisper. "Yes."

"Why, Andy? Why did Kathleen kill herself?"

"She'd found out she was pregnant."

"Thank you very much, Mr. Gordon."

Mercedes Cabbott's son shot to his feet and darted toward the door. Before Tully could move Andy was out of the house.

A moment later his car roared its belated defiance as it escaped.

Tully went into the utility washroom off the kitchen and plunged his face into a basinful of cold water. Then he went into the kitchen and looked up the number of the Pittman sanitarium and dialed it and asked if Mr. Oliver Hurst was still there, and how was Mrs. Hurst? He was told that Mr. Hurst had left not long before and sorry, we can give out no information about our patients.

Tully broke the connection, began to dial Ollie Hurst's home number, thought better of it, and hung up.

He got into the Imperial and drove over to the Hurst house.

Ollie answered the door. He looked like hell.

"Dave. I was just going to call you."

"How is Norma?"

"Quiet under sedation. The doctor kicked me out. Come on in. Something up?"

243

"Yes. I hate to ask this of you, Ollie — you look about as beat as I feel! — but would you do me a favor?"

"Don't be an idiot," Ollie Hurst said crossly. "What?"

"I'm going up to the Cabbott ménage to see Mercedes. I'd like you to be present when I tackle her."

"About what?"

"I'll explain later. Will you come?"

Ollie stood there. "You put me on a spot, Dave. I'm not comfortable in that house."

"I wish I could spare you," Tully said. "But Ollie, I've got to have you there."

"All right."

Ollie went for his jacket and tie. Tully got into his car and waited. Finally the lights went off and the lawyer came out and climbed in beside Tully. Tully turned the car around and headed for the hills.

As the Imperial turned into the Cabbott grounds Ollie Hurst said suddenly, "This isn't about Ruth, is it, Dave?"

"No."

"Then I don't see —"

"That is, not directly." Tully's mouth set in a grim line. "Everything I've been doing in the past few days has been about Ruth one way or the other, Ollie."

Hurst nodded and settled back. He appeared shrunken, half the size he had been.

It was George Cabbott who opened the door. The blond giant looked angry and formidable.

"We've been expecting you," Cabbott said. "Come in."

"Then you do know the story," Tully said.

"I do now!"

Mercedes's husband did not even glance at Oliver Hurst. He led them through the house to the terrace. Mercedes was waiting for them at the king-size terrace table. She looked odd in the weird lighting of the insect-repellent bulbs.

"It was quite horrid of you, David," Mercedes said in a high, tight voice.

"Yes," George Cabbott growled, "you sure had one hell of a nerve. Why don't you take me on for a change?"

"You didn't try to clobber me, George," Tully said. He looked around. A cigarette was smoldering in an ash tray on the table; neither Mercedes nor George Cabbott smoked. "I take it Andy's declared himself on the side of discretion. He's updated you, Mercedes?"

"My son felt he should tell me that you'd forced certain information from him," she said frigidly. "Did you have to trick him

245

into coming to your house?"

"And why Andy?" George Cabbott demanded. "If you wanted information, why didn't you ask Mercedes, like a man?"

"Do you think she'd have told me?"

"Of course I wouldn't have," Mercedes said. She had not once glanced Ollie Hurst's way. He stood just outside the circle of grisly light, a forlorn shadow.

"If you want to break a chain," Tully said sententiously, "choose the weakest link. Confucius or Sherlock Holmes or somebody, wasn't it?"

Mercedes poured herself a drink from the heavy silver cocktail shaker. Tully noted that her hands were trembling. She did not offer any to him or Hurst, or even ask them to sit down. She drank in hard gulps. Her husband stood by, watchful as a paid guard.

"All right, David. Now that you've broken the chain, what do you intend to do?"

"Get the rest of the story straight."

"Then the police?"

"I'm afraid so."

She poured another drink. George Cabbott took the glass from her hand and flung its contents out into the black lawn. She glanced at him, and he shook his head very slightly.

"How much will be made public, David?"

Tully shrugged. "The irreducible minimum, as far as I'm concerned."

"After all these years you'd destroy her image . . . blacken her name?"

"I can't destroy or blacken, Mercedes," Tully said. "That was done long ago, by others."

The beautiful young-old woman sank into a chair, her back growing a queer hump. Her husband leaned over and took her impeccable little hand. It lay there lifelessly.

"Why?" George Cabbott asked. "That's what I don't understand, Dave. What purpose does this serve?" He asked it in a determinedly reasonable tone, like a representative of management in a labor dispute.

"The cause of life, liberty and the pursuit of happiness," Tully replied. "My wife's."

Ollie Hurst stirred, stepped forward. In the light he looked like a ghost. "Dave. What did Andrew tell you?"

"The truth about Kathleen's death. When Mercedes strong-armed her into going abroad, Kathleen discovered that she was pregnant. She killed herself."

The lawyer stared at him. Then he shuffled over to the table and took the shaker and Mercedes's glass and poured. He set the shaker down carefully and drank slowly and thirstily. The tiniest frown appeared between Mercedes's graceful brows. "What else do you know, Dave?"

"You tell me, Ollie. Was Kathleen's child yours?"

"Yes."

"Did she know she was pregnant when her mother took her to Europe?"

"No. Kathleen wrote me from Switzerland. Her letter reached me after the news that she'd drowned. I knew she had committed suicide." Ollie Hurst stared out into the darkness.

"I suspected the baby was yours," Tully said thoughtfully. "If it had been Crandall Cox's —"

"You — shut — up," Mercedes Cabbott whispered. "You shut your filthy mouth!"

"If it had been Cox's," Tully said, "he'd have tried to cash in on it right away. Of course, he must have found out. How did he find out, do you suppose, Ollie?"

He saw the fine sweat appear on Hurst's bald head.

"The letter," Tully said softly. "Of course! The letter you just said Kathleen wrote you. Didn't you and Cox both go to college here? It must have been around the same time —"

"It was," Mercedes Cabbott said. "Oh, it was! And now I remember, Oliver. You and Crandall Cox roomed together during one semester."

"I'm going great guns, Ollie," Tully said. "I'm really hitting it now. That's it, sure. Cox swiped that letter from you, and he kept it like an insurance policy all these years. You probably thought you'd lost it. Isn't that it, Ollie?"

The lawyer said hoarsely, "Dave." He licked his lips and said again, "Dave."

But Tully said, "It was Kathleen's secret that brought Cranny Cox back here after fifteen years. He didn't come back to put the bite on you, Mercedes — he was desperate, and he'd saved that letter for a desperate day, but he knew how tough you could be, and he'd look for a softer touch.

"You, Ollie. You've done well for yourself — he'd have investigated *that* for sure. You're a respected member of the community. Your legal practice lies here. You have a vulnerable wife. He'd have played on all that, Ollie — counted on its making you pay through the nose to keep that letter from being published, ruining you socially, destroying your livelihood, maybe turning your wife into a hopeless lunatic.

"The one thing he didn't count on," Tully went on, and he had to steel himself with all his strength to keep from betraying the pity and sorrow and disgust he felt, "the one thing Cox didn't count on was the lengths to which you'd go to hold on to what he was threatening. And the fact that you're a lawyer and know that a blackmailer never stops.

"It was you who killed Cox, wasn't it, Ollie?"

20

The man with the shining bald head was silent. Suddenly he looked strange — older, thinner, less substantial. Mercedes Cabbott and her husband were regarding him as if they had never seen him before.

As perhaps they haven't, Tully thought.

"It would have been a pretty simple case if Cox hadn't been so greedy," Tully said into the silence, and then he shrugged. "But then he wouldn't have been Cox, would he? He came to town to blackmail you, Ollie, but while he was here he thought he'd do a little business with Sandra Jean, too . . . whom he knew as Ruth. He must have set up the appointment with Sandra Jean first — a little incidental he thought he'd get out of the way. I wondered why he didn't try to get some money out of Sandra on the spot — why he was willing to let her off the hook until she married Andy and he'd have something worth his while to go after. Now it's obvious. He didn't need Sandra's immediate pittance; he had a much bigger fish tugging on his line. So Sandra came and went, and then you came at *your* appointed time, Ollie."

He saw Ollie Hurst swallow, as if to gather sufficient moisture in his mouth to lubricate his voice. Before the lawyer could speak, Tully went on.

"You came, Ollie, and the gun Cox had taken away from Sandra was right there, and whether you came prepared to kill Cox or the sight of the gun set you off, you managed to grab it and cover him and wrap a towel around it and shoot him dead."

"And Ruth walked in on *that?*" Mercedes said in soft horror.

"She did, didn't she, Ollie?" Tully said. "She'd followed Sandra to the motel, seen her leave, saw you go into Cox's room, and she must have sensed that Cox had some hold on you, too. And with some quixotic idea of helping you — she's always liked and looked up to you, Ollie; you remember that, don't you? — Ruth barged into that room after you. And found you standing over Cox's dead body with the gun in your hand. It must have been your voice Maudie Blake heard calling Ruth by name, not Cox's — listening through that thin wall to the whole thing, Maudie must have made a lightning decision to lie for you and cover for you, Ollie, so that you'd have to pay *her* off. As you did, when you slipped into her room at Flynn's Inn subsequently and forced a lethal dose of booze down her drunken throat."

He was no longer Ollie Hurst at all, but a standing corpse, a breathing dead man, so still and stiff he might have been a corpse in fact. I wonder, Tully thought, if he even hears me now.

George Cabbott drew a quavery sort of breath and exhaled it noisily. "How do you know all this, Dave?"

"It follows from one simple thing, so simple I hardly noticed it at the time." Tully's breath came out under tension, too. "Ollie made a tremendous mistake. The night I went to Flynn's Inn at Maudie Blake's request, she told me she'd 'just' moved over there from the Hobby Motel. The next morning — the morning Ollie and I found her dead — we went in Ollie's car, Ollie driving. Never once the night before in Ollie's house, never once that morning in my house, did I mention the fact that Maudie Blake was no longer at the Hobby Motel, but had moved. And on the drive to Flynn's neither of us said a single word. *Yet Ollie drove directly to Flynn's Inn.*

"I didn't realize until much later how significant that was," Tully ground on. "In fact, I didn't remember it at all. Until, that is, I began to put the pieces together about Ollie's relationship fifteen years ago with Kathleen. Then it popped out, and it hit me between the eyes. That business with Kathleen concealed a possible motive for Ollie to have killed Cox. The knowledge he shouldn't have had — of where Maudie Blake had holed in — put him right smack in that room at Flynn's Inn — pouring a lethal dose of liquor down Maudie's gullet. It's not evidence, but I'm not after evidence — let Julian Smith and the prosecutor's office worry about that. In fact, what I'm after —"

"Dave," the corpse said. "Dave, you've got to understand I didn't know that gun belonged to you. All I saw was a gun — and that damn leering face . . . It was over — I was committed — before I really had time to think. And there he was, dead, and afterward that Blake horror — trying to squeeze me, too. . . ." Ollie Hurst said dully, "Didn't she realize that a man who's killed once finds it easy to kill a second time? I had to kill her. She knew. She knew everything."

"And Ruth?" Tully said. "And Ruth, Ollie?"

"Ruth . . . She walked in . . . I couldn't kill Ruth. Not Ruth. My friend. Norma's friend. Your wife. . . ."

Tully crouched slightly. He heard his breath whistling up from his lungs, tasted the foul taste of undiluted hatred in his mouth. "You couldn't kill Ruth, Ollie? Do you think you can still pull the old-pal act with me?" He dimly heard his own voice shouting. "You didn't kill Ruth then for one reason only: You needed her as your fall guy! And when you thought you were in the clear and you had Ruth all set up to take the rap for you — did you kill Ruth, too? *Did you, Ollie? Where did you put her? Where have you got her hidden? Alive or dead?*"

"Dave, no! I'll take him!"

It was George Cabbott who sprang between them, reaching for the lawyer with his bronze arms.

It was impossible, but Ollie Hurst moved faster. Tully saw the blur of his hand snatching the cocktail shaker from the table, the weirdly colored line of light it made as the shaker struck Cabbott squarely in the face. The big man went down with an expression of great surprise. Blood began to pump from his mouth.

And Ollie Hurst — portly, bald Ollie

Hurst — twisted his clumsy body and grabbed the terrace railing and vaulted over it like a gazelle and disappeared in the darkness.

Mercedes Cabbott dropped to her knees beside her husband with a faint cry.

Then Tully found himself on the black lawn, running.

He could not see Ollie, and he had to stop and listen for the thud of Ollie's feet on the turf. He ran, and stopped, and listened, and ran again. When the thudding sounds turned into snapping dry-stick sounds, Tully knew that the lawyer had reached the gravel driveway before the house and was sprinting across it.

How long he chased his quarry Tully had no notion. It seemed endless, and it seemed no time at all. He ran and stopped and ran like a man in a dream, where time did not exist.

At one point he made contact. He remembered seeing the flying figure suddenly, hearing the horrid labor of his lungs, launching himself into space from behind like a swimmer at the start of a race, watching Ollie beyond all reason twisting his chubby body sidewise in a slow-motion film, feeling his shoulder slam glancingly against Ollie's rib cage, pitching forward on his face with his hands extended to break his fall, feeling the jarring impact of his shoulder on the lawn, feeling himself tumbling over and coming to rest on his back, one vast windless pain.

The next thing David Tully became conscious of was running down a long slope after the fleeing lawyer. At the bottom of the slope stretched the Cabbott stables. His first reasoned thought came to him: Ollie Hurst had no plan, no destination. He was simply running, running in a blind instinct to prolong the sweet oblivion between crime and punishment. And he was dangerous. Now he was really dangerous.

Tully took longer strides. He was running easily now. It was no effort at all. He was only a few yards behind Ollie Hurst when the lawyer ducked into the hay-barn.

Tully plowed to a dead stop just outside the barn door. He listened, trying to hear over his own breathing. And he heard. He heard the huge and heaving gasps of an animal run to earth, incapable of further flight, cornered.

"Ollie," David Tully said. "Ollie, I'm coming in."

Nothing but the gasps.

"Don't try anything, Ollie. I'm not going

to hurt you. But you're going to tell me what I have to know."

There was a slobbering break in the gasps, and then they resumed.

Tully stood still.

Suddenly there was moonlight. It shone through the open door into the barn. He could not see Ollie from where he was standing.

"Ollie, I'm coming in."

Most of the barn was dark.

"Ollie?" Tully said. "Don't try to hide from me. I see you."

"No . . . you . . . don't."

Tully whirled. The gasping voice had come from behind him.

Ollie Hurst was crouched in the doorway. His torso was still heaving for oxygen, his mouth wide open, the moonlight bouncing off his teeth and wet skull and streaming cheeks. There was a pitchfork in his hands and its tines were a foot from Tully's throat.

"I don't want this, Dave," Ollie gasped. "I didn't ask for this. I've got to keep running as long as I can. The keys, Dave. Give me the keys to your car."

The shining needles of steel moved back and forth slightly, came closer.

Tully did not move. "Is Ruth alive?"

"Of course she's alive —"

"Where is she, Ollie? Where are you hiding her?" He wanted to believe. He so desperately wanted to believe.

"The keys," Ollie Hurst said again. "I'll get them one way or another, Dave. I'll get them if I have to kill you. Toss me those keys."

"Sure, Ollie. If you'll tell me where Ruth is."

"First the keys."

"No deal," Tully said. Was he lying? If Ruth were dead, wouldn't Ollie tell the hiding place in return for the keys without bargaining? He must be telling the truth . . .

And suddenly it came to him, as the other revelations had come to him, in a flash, whole and perfect. The tines were very close to his throat now, and he had to fight to ignore them.

"Or would this be it, Ollie? Where would an amateur like you find a hideout for your kidnap victim on the spur of the moment? You couldn't have made any preparations. It would have to exist — safe, isolated, ready for use.

"There's a place like that available to you, Ollie," Tully said, "the only place you could take her that fits the specifications. The place you and Norma call the old place, that Norma's great-grandfather built up in the hills. That's why you talked Norma out of going up there . . . The root-cellar would be a good spot. Ruth's in the root-cellar of the old place, isn't she, Ollie?"

The tines wavered. "Dave," Ollie Hurst said faintly. "Please —"

"George has phoned the police by this time, Ollie," Tully said. He felt as big and sure as a mountain. "Julian Smith . . . Ollie, listen! Hear it?"

It was the creeping hysteria of a police siren from far away.

"What's the use?" Tully asked the rigid man softly. "You'll only get yourself killed if you run. It isn't over by a damn sight, Ollie. Not while you've still got friends. Like me. And even Ruth. Give it to me?"

He carefully extended his hand.

Oliver Hurst collapsed. Everything gave way at once, head, arms, legs.

Tully took the pitchfork away from him.

"Ruth?"

He heard a gagged, frantic moan.

Tully smashed in the root-cellar door.

We hope you have enjoyed this Large Print book. Other Thorndike, Wheeler or Chivers Press Large Print books are available at your library or directly from the publishers.

For more information about current and up-coming titles, please call or write, without obligation, to:

Publisher
Thorndike Press
295 Kennedy Memorial Drive
Waterville, ME   04901
Tel. (800) 223-1244

Or visit our Web site at:
www.gale.com/thorndike
www.gale.com/wheeler

OR

Chivers Large Print
published by BBC Audiobooks Ltd
St James House, The Square
Lower Bristol Road
Bath BA2 3SB
England
Tel. +44(0) 800 136919
email: bbcaudiobooks@bbc.co.uk
www.bbcaudiobooks.co.uk

All our Large Print titles are designed for easy reading, and all our books are made to last.